Totally Bound Publishing books by Nikki McCoy:

Everything That You Are
My Forever
Shattered Heart

Keepers of the Gods
Son of Death
Master of Wrath
Keepers of the Night
Slave to Chaos

Of Blood and Spirit
Crimson Mate

I0617790

SHATTERED HEART

NIKKI MCCOY

SHATTERED HEART

Dedication

A special thanks to my editors for their patience, my friends and family for their love and support and all those trying to find sanity in an insane world! It's a never-ending quest full of heartache, mystery and the occasional miracle, but it's also life, and I wouldn't have it any other way.

Chapter One

Corin yanked the wrench one last quarter turn, sat back on his heels and wiped the sweat from his brow. The elbow drainpipe under the sink was like nearly everything else that held together the dilapidated hotel—deteriorated and well past the point of usefulness. He was sure the building would have been condemned long ago if there were any regulations in effect to deem it a hazard. As it was, any fool could run a business from a cardboard box, so long as the customers shelled out the green and the property rent was paid each month.

Standing, he turned on the faucet and peered underneath again. When he was confident that the leak was fixed—for now—he gathered his tools and placed them in the rusted toolbox at his side. A glance at the clock on the wall showed that it was almost time for him to head to the front desk and close up shop, but if he was quick, he could squeeze in one more job. Not that it would make a difference.

He was so far behind in his duties, a beating was inevitable. It could be disputed that there was more maintenance needed than he had time to accomplish each day, but he'd made that mistake once and had learned his lesson painfully.

Corin shut off the lights on his way out, pausing in the corridor when static came through on his portable radio. Madeline's voice rose above it, but only barely.

"Cory, I have a gentleman that wants to speak to a manager. Could you come here, please?"

Corin gripped the toolbox firmly and rushed the length of the threadbare carpet to the end of the hall. There were only two reasons why she would call for a manager, and from her high-pitched tone, he doubted that it was at the customer's insistence. He took the exit that led to a walkway curving around the faded brick exterior of the building and re-entered through the back door of the laundry room. After discarding the toolbox onto a metal rack, he wove around a clutter of boxes and large clothes bins to the door on the other side.

As soon as he was through, Madeline crashed into him and he braced her steadily against him. Her petite body trembled in his hands as she looked up, chocolate-colored eyes wide with fright. Just as she opened her mouth, a taunting bellow came from the other side of the partition between the office and the front desk.

"Hey, c'mon back here, cupcake. I wasn't done talkin' to you yet."

Corin grabbed the set of keys from his belt and quickly unlocked the office door. Pushing his sister inside, he whispered, "Lock this and don't come out 'til I say so."

Madeline nodded in earnest and did as she was told, leaving the light off inside. She knew the drill, and he trusted her to stay safe until the issue was resolved.

Hopefully, this would turn out to be a good night, one in which violence wasn't the first resort. Summoning a façade of confidence and a neutral expression, he walked around to the desk and assessed the situation with a practiced eye. There was only one man in the lobby who straightened from where he leaned over the counter and gave Corin a once-over. His dirt-caked clothes looked as if they'd fallen from the sky and landed on him. The putrid odor contaminating the air spoke of days, if not weeks, of hygiene neglect, although he didn't appear to be wasted on drugs or alcohol. Always a plus.

The man screwed up his wrinkled face. "Who the hell are you?"

Edging his way to the far right side of the desk and the aluminum bat hidden beneath the counter, Corin replied, "I'm the manager. Is there something I can do for you?" A little closer. The knob on the bat glinted dully within sight from its position against the wall.

"Yeah, you can give me a room with that sweet little cat in it." The man licked his lips then tipped his head in the direction Madeline had run.

Anger thrummed to the forefront of Corin's thoughts at the lewd request. It wasn't the first time a man had lusted after his sister, and it was hardly the best attempt, but it still drew out every protective instinct he possessed. Madeline was only fifteen, for Christ's sake! Though her body was maturing in ways too obvious to conceal, there could be no mistaking her for a fully developed woman, and it was apparent that she wasn't a slave. No collar circled her neck and no brands marked her body, yet that seemed to mean next to nothing when it came to most men's hormones and their lack of inhibitions. He, more than most, knew that age was rarely taken into consideration by men like the one in front of him, and it filled him with disgust.

"She's not for sale. If you want a room, it's twenty dollars a night."

The man narrowed his gaze and sneered, displaying a full row of rotted teeth. "And what if I just want her?"

"You'll have to go through me first." He gripped the bat in one hand, but kept it from view of the stranger. There was a lot to be said for the element of surprise.

A raucous laugh burst from the guy and he spat out, "You? I could crush you like a bug. What are you, a buck ten soaking wet?"

Corin ignored the insult. He knew his size was nothing to be intimidated by—however, that didn't mean he was without resources. "If you don't leave now, I'll have to make you." He tightened his grip, letting the man see the flexing of his biceps. With any luck, what was in his hand would be mistaken for a gun. Sometimes it worked. Other times...

Corin's heart rate spiked when the man suddenly jumped forward and slammed his hands onto the counter in a scare tactic. More laughter rang out as Corin lurched back, despite his effort to remain in control.

"You're lucky I ain't into boys, or I'd show you how that piece you got can be used for something other than killing."

It wasn't until the man had sauntered off and the double entry doors had swung closed behind him that Corin managed to draw his next breath. Slumping against the wall, he released the bat and willed his heart to stop racing.

But it never had a chance to do so.

Corin's lungs froze as Scott stumbled through the doors with a pint of whiskey in hand and a rolled cigarette hanging from slack lips. Black hair flecked with gray clung to his sweat-filmed forehead and he leaned into every step as if on the brink of toppling over, though Corin knew the deceptiveness of that gait. Unlike with most people, alcohol only sharpened Scott's reflexes, giving him liquid strength as well as courage that brought out his true, sadistic nature.

Corin pressed farther into the wall as he glared at the man through the veil of his shoulder-length, white-blond hair. Promising thoughts of torture and murder filled his mind and lent him comfort. One day, he'd coat his hands with that man's blood and spit in his face as he lay dying with no one to mourn his passing. He would make it slow, drawing his death out for as long as possible and dance to the sweet music of his cries for mercy.

"Boy!"

Corin started, realizing belatedly that Scott was now behind the desk and advancing on him with focused intent. At the last moment he remembered to avert his eyes, his hand twitching with the urge to reach for the fallen baseball bat.

"Have you finished all your chores yet?" Scott lumbered forward until his bulky frame eclipsed most of the overhead light.

A lie played on the tip of Corin's tongue, but he swallowed it down. If there was one thing his stepfather was meticulous about, it was keeping account of his failures. Anything to give the man the opportunity to punish him—to be alone with him for a few hours. His list of chores would be checked in the morning and lying would only make the consequences worse.

"No, sir."

Pain exploded in his right eye as knuckles cracked along its edge. Corin tensed against the reflex to raise his arms in protection. That would only serve to piss the man off more.

"Worthless. I should've killed you at birth." Scott took a swig from his fifth, put it on the countertop then clasped Corin's throat and slammed him back against the wall. The fetid stench of his breath as he leaned in close assaulted Corin's nostrils, causing bile to churn in his stomach. "You're only good for one thing and we both know what that is."

"Dad?"

Scott jerked back so suddenly, Corin nearly fell forward, gasping for lost breath. "Madeline, what are you doing here? Where's your mom?" He cast a guilty look around then snatched up the bottle.

"She's in bed. Should I tell her you're home?"

"No," he said a little too quickly. "No need to wake her. I was just headed to bed myself."

Corin caught the look of postponed violence aimed at him before Scott ambled away through the lobby and down the main corridor. A fine tremor racked Corin's bones as he struggled to regain his composure. When it was possible, he stretched his spine, only to hiss as Madeline jabbed two fingers at the bruise already forming by his right eye.

"Addie!"

"Why do you let him do that to you?"

Oh, God. "Don't start this again, Addie. Not now." He walked stiffly around the partition and into the office with Madeline dogging his heels.

"Why not now? You think I don't know what's going on? I'd have to be blind not to notice."

Corin flipped the switch to turn off the outside lights, sighed and physically moved his sister from his path to the front doors.

"You can't spend the rest of your life being his punching bag. Why are you so afraid to stand up to him?"

Humiliation rooted his feet to the scuffed tile floor. He let his head fall back and took a moment to gather his patience as another piece of his dwindling pride perished. They'd had this conversation dozens of times, but it never got easier. And why should it? She was naïve and innocent because he kept her that way. She didn't need to know about the threats her father made if Corin ever dared to leave or the extent of their mother's hatred for him. If his sacrifices kept her and Amy safe, then that was all that mattered. Better they think him a coward than to allow the alternative to happen.

Corin willed his feet into motion and locked the deadbolts then wrapped the thick chain on one of the doors around both handles to secure it with a padlock. "Addie, I've got a lot of work to do and you need to get to bed."

"I know you think you have to stay to protect us," she said, following him back to the office, "but he's not going to hurt us. He never has."

"Addie, stop." He walked to a single filing cabinet and pulled out several labeled manila folders.

"I just don't see why you're throwing your life away by staying here. I mean, I'll miss you and all, but we'll see each other again. When I turn eighteen, I'll find you and we'll both wait for Amy." When he didn't respond, she huffed in frustration. "Do you like what he does to you? Do you like it when—"

Corin slammed the cabinet drawer closed and squeezed his eyes shut at the return of his anger that carried with it a heavy dose of self-loathing. Over the years, he'd fallen into the convenient routine of ignoring the situation, pretending that as long as his sisters remained unaware, it didn't exist. It seemed now that comforting escape was no longer an option. Scott was getting bolder, more careless, and it wouldn't be much longer before Amy also began to see beyond the thin veneer of his farce.

How much was he really protecting them when he was powerless himself? He had to do something—and soon. Problem was, there was no conceivable resolution that might lead to a better outcome. If he killed Scott, he was positive he could manage the hotel on his own, but his mother would never allow that. She would either try to take revenge or kick him out. If he took his sisters and ran, he'd be putting them at risk of kidnapping and enforced slavery. In a world where the only laws were the ones made at the business end of a gun and the cold exchange of hard cash, he was severely lacking.

Taking a deep breath, he turned around and cringed inwardly at the thick tears brimming Madeline's lashes. When he opened his arms, she ran into them and hugged his waist tightly.

"I'm afraid for you, Cory."

He squeezed back, closing his eyes on an exhale. "It'll be all right, I promise. Now, go to bed. We've got nearly a full house, so Mom will be waking you up early to help her with the rooms."

Madeline sniffed, rubbed her cheeks on his shirt then kissed him lightly. "Love you," she whispered as she started for her room.

Corin stared down at the residue of her tears on his T-shirt before scraping a hand through his hair. It would be all right. He would find a way to make things better, no matter how long it took.

While the outdated computer on the laminate desktop booted up, he put on a fresh pot of coffee and settled in for the night audit and AR paperwork. This was his favorite part of the job—no interruptions, no debasing expectations, no people. His body was his own temple, and his mind could lose itself in the figures. About an hour into it, however, his brain decided to shut off. Corin snapped out of a daze he hadn't known he'd fallen into and blinked for, apparently, the first time in a while. His eyes stung and welled instantly at the return of moisture and he couldn't seem to scrub the grit from them.

Exhaustion clawed at his muscles and sapped every ounce of his waning strength. His stomach gurgled as it ate itself, screaming for sustenance other than water and caffeine, even as the thought of food made him nauseated. He was well past the point of hunger and trying to force down a few stolen scraps from the kitchen would only succeed in luring him to sleep, which he couldn't afford. Scott had been going out every day for almost a week, piling his workload onto Corin and expecting nothing short of perfection. It wasn't uncommon, but this period had lasted longer than usual and it had left him feeling weak, both physically and mentally. Pushing four days of next to no sleep, he was going to crash soon—and hard.

Corin palmed the edge of the desk, pushed the rolling chair back and stood up. After a quick glance around, he started rifling through the drawers of the desk, filing cabinet and extra storage containers. Scott had to have a bottle of poppers hidden somewhere.

They were the man's last defense against the worst of his hangovers and better than any energy drink out there.

Under a stack of last year's revenue spreadsheets, he came across an envelope filled with color photographs. Curiosity got the better of him and he sat down on the floor to shuffle through them. Scott and his mother, Doreen, starred in most of them, only they appeared to be over three decades younger than they were now. Color prints, *any prints,* should have been next to impossible to procure at that time. Though Corin had never gone to school, he knew that period had marked the start of the riots that had followed the devastation of mankind.

There was no proof as to which country had initiated the biochemical warfare that had decimated more than one-third of the human population. Alliances between countries had obligated even the most reluctant of governments to get involved until not a single nation on earth had remained immune to the effects of the ten year war. In the ensuing aftermath, chaos had reigned. Looting and riots had plunged all but the upper class into poverty, and medical facilities and supplies had become nonexistent for those without a fortune to buy them.

Diseases had swept through the remaining populace and further reduced the number of people on the planet, until finally a new order of law had been erected. Not quite new, exactly. He'd been told once that history was merely repeating itself—that there had once before been widespread slavery and extreme measures of lawlessness such as there was now. The elderly man who'd spoken of those times had oddly seemed as though he recalled them fondly. As if the previous measures of slavery in human history were preferable to him than the laws that were currently in effect.

Even though Corin was too young to know anything other than the conditions he'd been born into, he couldn't help but imagine what it must have been like before the war. What his life might have been like had it never taken place. Corin snorted. If not for the war, he wouldn't even exist. He should never have existed, as his mother took great pains to remind him every chance she got.

Corin feathered a thumb over Doreen's smiling face in the photograph. She looked so happy and young. She couldn't have been more than eighteen at the time, standing beside a Scott he almost couldn't recognize for the blissful contentment on his youthful features. The hotel stood proudly behind them with a fresh coat of paint and green lawns surrounding it.

If Corin had assumed their ages correctly, the decade of warfare had just ended and the decade of darkness, as most people called it, had begun. Scott and Doreen had decided to hold off on having children until they felt it safe. After some semblance of order had been incorporated by those strong enough to hold it, and the laws of slavery set into action, the happy couple had tried for three years with no luck. Until one night when Doreen had been gang-raped by a group of thugs while Scott had been away. Unable to afford an abortion and after several failed attempts to kill the baby in her womb via drugs and starvation, Corin had been born.

While his mother had wanted to sell him into slavery immediately, Scott had convinced her that they could use him as their own slave. Why pay for an extra hand when they'd gained one for free? Not quite free, however. Doreen despised him with a passion that was in direct opposition to the love she held for her two daughters. Though Corin had nearly died many times from her neglect, there was goodness in her. Every day he saw it in the way she treated Amy and Madeline, and for that, he could never truly hate her as she did him.

The patter of muffled footsteps brought him back to awareness and he shoved the pictures away, heart pounding with guilt as he jumped up. Relief quickly flooded him when he saw it was only Amy stepping hesitantly into the office. Her auburn curls were mussed around her cherubic face and a worn, once-blue cotton blanket was clutched in her small hands. At six years old, she was the exact replica of Madeline at that age and, likewise, had him wrapped around her little finger.

Corin scooped her up and sat with her in his lap. Her large, caramel-colored eyes were shaded with fright as they peered up at him. Smoothing silky wisps from her face, he asked, "What's wrong, baby girl? Couldn't sleep?"

Amy shook her head and whispered, "Mommy and Daddy are fighting again. They sound really mad."

With an ease born of necessity and experience, he plastered on a calming smile and pulled her closer to mask the trembling in his hands. "I'm sure it's not that serious. Nothing the sun won't cure tomorrow." Amy bobbed her little head, but her forlorn expression remained. "Do you want to stay with me for a bit? I can tell you the story about the elves that lived in the forest with their magical princess."

His sister's face brightened with the radiance of a white-toothed grin. "Really?"

Corin nodded. With Scott still awake, he risked the man's fury if he was discovered keeping Amy with him this late at night, but her comfort always superseded the repercussions. After resituating her in his lap and tucking the blanket around her small frame, he settled back, smiling faintly as Amy rested her head on his shoulder. He wove a tale of mystery and fantasy—dreams of things he'd only read about such as lush trees, wealth and kindness amongst strangers. Magics that took place far away from the ravaged and barren landscape they lived in.

Long after Amy had fallen asleep, he continued to give life through his imagination until the constriction of his chest choked the words from his mouth.

Scott had been going out consistently over the past week, and his arguing with Doreen could only mean one thing. That he'd gambled and boozed away their profits again. Winter was coming, and the cold season would slow business significantly over the next several months. Without the benefit of profits to see them through, they would starve, but this was hardly the first time Scott had put his own needs above those of his family. And they had never starved, not with Corin there to make up for what was lost.

He absently wondered how long it would take him to work back the money this time, and how often he would be sold before it was over. Corin laughed humorlessly while fighting to keep the despair from pulling him under. There was no end to the cycle. He was a slave for all intents and purposes, tethered as securely as if he wore the proof around his neck. If he ever resisted subservience, Madeline would be next in line to suffer the faults of her father, and he would never allow that to happen.

Pressing a kiss to the crown of Amy's curls, he leaned over the desk and dialed Madeline's room. She answered on the fourth ring, a tint of irritation coloring her tone.

"Hey, I'm bringing Amy up now."

There was a short pause, then, "Crap, I'm sorry. I didn't even realize she was gone. Is everything okay?"

"Yeah. Just had a nightmare or something. I'll be there in a few."

After another period of silence, she asked tentatively, "They were fighting again, weren't they? I don't hear them now."

Corin repressed a sigh of relief. Madeline and Amy's room was right next to their parents', and with no sign of Scott and the absence of noise from his room, his stepfather had most likely passed out for the night. "They're probably asleep. I'll see you soon."

"'Kay."

Corin hung up and carried Amy to her room where Madeline waited tiredly at the door. He bade Madeline goodnight then trudged back to the office, his search for the poppers forgotten. He had no need for them anymore, not with the fear-laced adrenaline pumping through his system. With renewed vigor, he attacked his duties and lost himself once again in the mindless configuration of numbers.

Chapter Two

The steady drone of maintenance work that filled the hours of the next day did nothing to ease Corin's frayed nerves. The slightest sound made him jump, and around every corner he expected to find Scott lurking in wait. Although the man had taken off sometime in the late morning, sleep deprivation obscured Corin's lucidity and he found no relief in his stepfather's absence. Instead, anticipation of what the night might hold threatened to unravel his semblance of control. The waiting was always more torture than what was coming to him, and he couldn't shake the feeling that this time would be worse than the others.

Madeline met him at noon with a bowl of bland chicken broth sprinkled with broken crackers. When Corin turned it away politely, his belly roiling objectionably at the idea of consuming it, Madeline sat and refused to leave until he agreed to at least try to eat. He quickly relented — not because it would appease his sister, but because he didn't want to get caught distracting Madeline from her chores. Doreen had been watching him all morning and wouldn't hesitate with a punishment if she saw them together.

Corin scarfed down as much as he could stomach, which was only half, then handed the rest back. Eventually, Madeline gave up on trying to convince him to eat more and left him alone. An hour before he was scheduled to relieve her at the front desk to start on the night audit, his radio crackled to life and Scott's brusque summons came through. Swallowing his nervousness, he gathered his tools and headed to the front where he found his stepfather sitting on a tall stool behind the counter.

Without so much as a glance in his direction, Scott handed him a plastic key card and said, "Room twenty-three. Clean yourself up first."

"Yes, sir." Corin took the card and left, exiting the hotel from the back entrance and heading for the toolshed that doubled as his living quarters. It was small, confined and contained more junk than space to move around in. The wires that had once supplied electricity to it had long since eroded, and the luxury of heat had never graced its insides. His only personal possessions consisted of a thin, vinyl-covered mattress on the cement floor covered by a ratted, wool blanket, a small collection of books left behind by previous guests adorning a two-shelf metal rack and a few paintings Madeline had given to him in secret for two of his previous birthdays.

Though he'd seen no other art with which to compare her works, aside from the redistributed prints hanging in the rooms of the hotel, her talent was more than apparent in her creations. Each night, he pulled them out of a corner where Scott never bothered to look and propped them against the floor-to-ceiling shelves lining the wall opposite his bed. He would stare at the beauty of the brushstrokes and marvel at the fluent artistry in the glow of flickering candlelight.

Except for nights like this.

With single-minded focus, he placed the toolbox in its designated spot and grabbed a spare set of clothes from the stand at the foot of his mattress. Tucking them under one arm, he locked the shed behind him and went back to the hotel. The halls were thankfully empty of his sisters and guests and he hurried to room twenty-three to close himself within. In a matter of minutes, he was undressed and standing underneath the warm spray of the showerhead in the bathroom, with his clothes folded neatly in the bottom drawer of the dresser.

As he methodically washed every inch and crevice of his body, his mind gradually sank into the familiar mentality of acceptance. Gone was the anticipation of surprise, and in its place was the strangely assuring knowledge of what was expected of him. His stepfather was sure to have found more than one person to contribute to the restoration of his gambling expenditures, but at least the wait was over. The sooner he started, the sooner he would finish.

Until the next time.

Corin stepped from the narrow stall and used the blow dryer on his hair, after drying his body with a towel. He shaved and brushed his teeth with efficiency then cleaned the bathroom when he was through, stuffing the evidence of his grooming next to his clothing in the dresser. Afterwards, he knelt on the carpeted floor with his hands clasped behind his back and head bent submissively, as Scott had trained him to do long ago.

It wasn't long before a clamoring in the hallway heralded the arrival of the men he would service for the night, only it wasn't two sets of shuffling footsteps that neared the door nor two boisterous voices breaking the silence of the hour. Dread curled in his gut when the door opened and several pairs of mud-covered boots came into view of his lowered gaze. Fear renewed itself as he counted four…no, five pairs of legs gathering around him.

He'd been prepared for two men, three at the most, as was the usual, but Scott had apparently hit the jackpot earlier in the day. There had only been one other time that Corin had serviced a group so large and the memory was enough to send a shudder coursing down his spine.

"Damn, he is a pretty one," said a gruff voice from above. "The owner wasn't lyin', but I don't see a slave collar 'round his neck."

A hand reached down to roughly angle Corin's head to the side so that they could inspect his neck through the fall of his hair. The man holding him grunted then released his jaw. "So what? He's ours for the night. Bought and paid for. Damn, look at that mouth." He pushed two fingers from each hand past Corin's lips and wrenched his jaw open as far as it would go. "I can't wait to get lost in there."

A round of laughter followed the comment, as well as several large hands groping and fondling what they could reach of Corin's kneeling form. The strong odors filling the air of leather, alcohol and bodies gone too long without the basic necessities competed with lustful remarks and challenges. Corin kept his eyes on the floor, gritting his teeth and doing his best to hold still against the numerous slaps and pinches they delivered.

"Get him warmed up," one of the men called from the vicinity of the bathroom. "I want him nice and loose by the time I get out."

"Don't you worry 'bout that none," the man who'd assaulted his mouth said. "We're gonna split this boy wide open. Jerry, hand me that joint and get them condoms out."

The multiple hands groping him disappeared and Corin used that break to risk a quick glance around the room. Two of the men looked to be in their late twenties with decently built frames and tan lines that marked their arms, legs and foreheads where their bandanas probably rode most of the time. The third was middle-aged with a slightly bulging abdomen, same as the fourth who appeared to be made of more hair than skin. The bow in their legs and the accumulated mud on their jeans signified their status as seasoned bikers. The floor was soon littered with clothes, as each man stripped and kicked their piles to the side.

Corin's attention snapped back to the hairy beast in front of him when the man sat on the nearest twin bed and yanked him over by his hair. With no small effort, he cleared the wince from his features and resumed his expression of neutrality. Scott charged well for his services, which entailed more than simply a hole to find release in. A good majority of the clientele wanted the act as well, not just the fuck. Some of them preferred a slave eager to please and begging for their manhood, while others enjoyed the thrill of inflicting pain, taking pleasure in seeing how far they could go before he broke.

Corin had a sickening hunch that this group of men belonged to the latter category.

A thick cock protruding from a coarse, dark bush of pubes wagged in front of his face as he maneuvered his body in between the man's thighs. He kept his mouth closed and his eyes down, obediently awaiting the man's commands. A good slave never took the initiative. Their every movement was choreographed by their Master or Mistress, according to his or her whims—down to the very sounds they were given permission to make. Slaves were no more than the instrument of their owner's passion.

Corin repeated the lessons Scott had beaten into him over and over again in his head, trying to control his rising panic. There were so many of them, and memories of the last time he'd submitted to more than two men at once prevailed over his determination to remain detached.

An open palm slapped him smartly across the cheek. "Open up, bitch. Jerry, what the hell's taking so long?"

Corin unclenched his jaw and opened his mouth, breaths coming in short, uneven pants. The sound of foil tearing reached his ears before a torn condom wrapper was thrown to the floor beside him. Callused hands jerked him up by his hips, positioning him on all fours. They pried the mounds of his ass apart and the cold dribble of lube down his exposed entrance caused the sensitive muscles there to contract.

"I'm ready," the man behind him said, as the blunt tip of his cock nudged insistently at Corin's bud. "On three. One, two…"

Searing pain tore through him with ferocious intensity when the man at his back thrust brutally forward. The scream gathering in his lungs was cut off by the significant length of the hairy beast's steel erection plunging into his mouth and taking root at the back of his throat. With two unyielding fists knotted in his hair, his lips were held at the base of the beast's crotch while the other man rammed into him with a fury that stole the breath from his lungs. Agony lanced along his nerves as his muscles contracted, his skin torn apart on the outside while his insides were punched repeatedly.

He couldn't breathe, couldn't move, could barely think past the misery of the relentless pummeling. His ears thundered with mounting pressure and his chest heaved in useless attempts to draw in precious air. Acid burned at the back of his throat and his insides shifted under the torrent of the man's frenzy. Corin knew what was about to happen as soon as the beast raised his fists to slam his mouth back down again, but was helpless to prevent it. His stomach, already weak from malnourishment, convulsed violently under the combined assault and hurled its displeasure immediately after the fifth downward tug from the beast. Bile spewed forth, and though Corin was able to swallow most of it, there was still enough expelled for the beast to notice.

"Shit! He just puked all over me. Hold up, man."

His belly cramped again as the man behind him pulled out abruptly. The beast threw Corin off and he slumped to the floor, spitting out the last of the acid scorching his tongue. Horror at what he'd just done drenched his entire being and through gasping breaths, he choked out, "I'm sorry. I'm—"

New pain blazed through him as a foot drove into his unprotected gut. Another kick rolled him onto his back and the beast's sneering face leaned down to fill his swimming vision.

"Seems we need to teach you a few lessons."

"Aw, c'mon, Parker. I was just about to get off."

"Shut it!" the beast growled. "We got all night to play with him, but he needs to learn some manners first." His beady eyes scrutinized Corin's quivering form for several moments then crinkled with a malicious grin. "Hand me that bottle over there. Chester, hold him down."

It was only the years of ruthless training he'd endured that enabled him to repress the urge to retreat from Chester's advance. The older man yanked Corin up onto his knees and took up position at his back. He wrapped one long arm around Corin's arms and torso, trapping him against his chest, and used his free hand to grip Corin's hair and wrench it back. The beast's bearded face took the place of the ceiling in Corin's view as fingers dug into the joints of his jaw, prying it open.

"This'll help you loosen up."

Corin squeezed his eyes shut while a bottle was inserted into his mouth and liquid fire poured down his raw throat. When he coughed some of it up, someone pinched his nostrils and he had no choice but to swallow the contents, hoping he didn't drown under the force of the flow. The liquor hit his empty stomach with the power of a semi and by the time they released him, the room was spinning wildly, a whirlwind beyond his control.

"Get him on the bed. Use these."

More hands bore into his flesh hard enough to leave bruises and hefted him, belly-side down, onto the bed. Coarse rope was bound to his wrists and ankles and stretched him taut over the surface of the sheeted mattress. Seconds passed in which Corin tried to catch his breath, but it exploded from his lungs on a scream as fire arced across his back.

"Plug up his mouth. Yeah, that'll work. Can't have too much noise or the owner will keep our deposit."

That from the beast—or possibly someone else. Corin couldn't be sure with the world tilting on its axis like an out of control wrecking ball. A small bundle of foul-smelling fabric was stuffed into his mouth and secured with a cord, which was tied at the base of his skull. In the next moment, the fire resumed and flamed across the skin of his back in excruciating, systematic lashes. They traversed the length of his shoulders, back, ass and thighs from top to bottom and back again. Muffled cries and pleas for mercy turned to incoherent sobs not even he heard above the roaring pain that consumed every fiber of his being.

Dimly, he became aware of hands shuffling him around, resituating him so that he lay on his back with his head lolling over the side of the bed and his mouth hanging open, free of its binding. His knees were pulled up to his chest and this time, when he was entered from both ends, there was no reactive struggle. The cocks slid in without resistance, thrusting vigorously until he was filled with the heat of their release.

They used him long into the night and past the early morning hours, each one taking a turn at his battered holes while the others showered and rested. Each time they caught him fading into unconsciousness, they found means with which to keep him awake. Toys from their saddlebags and various instruments around the room were used to invade his body and prolong their entertainment. One man seemed to have an obsession with his soft penis and took great pleasure in slapping it viciously and repeatedly whenever Corin failed to give an eager response to the liberties taken with his body.

His only indication that the group was finally readying to depart was the frenzy with which they attacked him again. They held him down, as if he had the strength to protest, and lunged into both ends, each man setting up a furious pace, as though trying to get the most out of what they had paid for. And they did. Corin lay sprawled afterwards across the rumpled sheets of the bed without even the energy to tuck in his arms and legs for warmth. His thoughts were tangled in a haze of torment and his head throbbed with the aftermath of a vicious hangover.

And that was how Scott found him that morning.

Through the cracks in his lids, he watched his stepfather sneer in disgust then leave the room. Sometime later, the man returned with a smile that practically radiated satisfaction.

"Apparently, you were good to them. Real good. They paid me double what I asked 'em for. Gonna be a week before I can rent you out again, but it was worth it. Get cleaned up and back to work. Madeline will be here in an hour to inspect the room."

Corin waited until he was alone once again then slowly made his way, inch by agonizing inch, to the bathroom. The side of the bed seemed to sneak up on him and he tumbled bunglingly to the floor. Fortunately, he landed on his face instead of his back and managed to gain his knees and hands with minimal effort. Only the thought of his sister walking in and finding him—and the dozen or more used condoms scattered across the floor—pushed him through the labor of his routine.

He showered, using one of the half-empty bottles of shampoo for soap, and bit through one side of his tongue while he eased his fresh set of clothes over pelted flesh. The belt the beast had used on him had been made of stiff, braided leather with sharp edges that had sliced open his skin in more than a few places. The fabric of his clothing smeared the trickles of blood, but there was no time to worry about that. With the window open to let in a chill breeze, he collected all of the trash from the floor and sealed it in an opaque laundry bag. He filled a second with the dirty sheets and his clothes from last night, making one last sweep of the room before leaving it.

The limp in his step was due not so much to the stretch of his skin, but from the clawing ache just below his midriff, deep inside his gut. He'd been feeling that empty cramping a lot lately, especially after encounters with some of the particularly brutal men who used him, but it had never been as intense as this. His insides felt as if someone had taken a spoon to them and left him barren. Brief panic flared and passed just as quickly at the idea that serious damage had been done. The only form of medicine available to him was antibacterial soap. If there were injuries that required anything more than that, they would just have to heal on their own.

He was almost to the exit, almost clear, when Madeline's voice called out to him. He hid the bags behind his back as his sister bustled around the corner, leaving a large cart with cleaning supplies to rush over to him.

"Cory! Why are you hunched over like that? Is something wrong?" She tried to push back his hair to get a better look at his face.

Corin batted her hands away. "I'm f-fine, just sick."

Madeline peered closer with her usual persistence and gasped. "Your lips are swollen and bleeding. Did Scott do that to you?"

"Didn't finish my chores yesterday." Corin let her make her own assumptions about the half-truth. Thankfully, she took that as a sufficient explanation.

"Is your stomach bothering you again?"

"I'll be all right. Go on back—"

"Madeline!" The sharp crack of their mother's voice made him cringe back a step. Doreen gave him a cool once-over before turning her full attention to her daughter. "Go help Amy in the kitchen for a minute, will you? I'm afraid she burnt the oatmeal again."

Madeline chewed on her bottom lip with an objection in her expressive eyes as her stare toggled between Doreen and Corin, but she let it go. "Sure, Mom."

Corin kept his gaze on the floor while Madeline walked away, knowing better than to leave until he was given permission.

"You're late," Doreen said coldly. "I won't tolerate that sort of behavior. Get your tools and start immediately."

"Y-yes, ma'am." His mother spun on her heel and walked briskly after Madeline, leaving Corin to make his way out to the shed to pick up his tools. He threw the bag with his clothes in it onto his bed then tossed the other into the dumpster outside. The rest of the day dragged on interminably. With alcohol still in his veins and blood constantly fusing his clothes to his skin as it dried, only to seep out again when the welts reopened with each stretch, it was an ongoing battle to keep his body in motion. Scott had promised him a week to heal before he was sold again, but that didn't mean he wouldn't be punished for dereliction of his duties—or that his stepfather would keep his word.

While kneeling in a tub to replace the seal to the drain, his vision suddenly blurred with a wave of dizziness. He leaned his forehead onto the rim of the tub and closed his eyes. Just a moment's rest. That was all he needed. Corin sighed, readjusted his weight on the hard porcelain and was out in the next second.

Chapter Three

"Cory!"

Corin jerked awake, heart hammering with the fear of getting caught asleep on the job. Madeline tugged on his arm insistently, trying to pull him out of the tub he was in. How long had he been asleep?

"You've got to come now! They're hurting him."

With a hiss and a grimace, he stood and stepped gingerly out of the tub. The pounding in his head had been replaced by the sore burn of stiff muscles. If it were possible, the cramping in his gut had become worse. If he'd been able to breathe right then, he was certain he would have cried out.

"Cory, come on!"

"Addie," he gritted through clenched teeth, "what are you talking about?"

The tracks of tears stained her flushed cheeks and her lower lip quivered as she sucked in air. "The rent collectors are here and they've brought more men with them. They're beating Dad up because he doesn't have the money. They're hurting him!"

Then why the hell would I want to interfere? Corin clamped his lips shut before that could slip out. For all Madeline was aware of some of the tortures Scott subjected him to, she still loved her father. After all, she'd never been the object of his hatred.

"Please," Madeline begged, turning the full weight of her desperate charm on him.

Corin sighed shallowly then followed her from the room and down the path leading to the back entrance of the laundry room. If anything, it should be a good show. *And maybe they'll do my job for me and kill him.* The thought sent a bolt of excitement down his spine and urged him to walk faster. The idea was highly improbable. One couldn't collect debts from a dead man and if Scott lived, Corin would be the first outlet he used to vent his anger, but it would be worth it to see his stepfather brought down a few notches.

Doreen's frantic cries could be heard above the deeper voices of several men. Madeline preceded him to the front area behind the desk where he stopped to take in the scene before him. Two thugs held Scott by the arms as Tully, the powerfully built black man who came to garner their rent every month, was taking his time punching his victim in the stomach. A gold knuckle ring flashed on his hand each time he brought it back to deliver another blow. A third thug stood to the side with a screaming and kicking Doreen held securely against his chest.

Watching all of this from several paces away were the men who'd recently started coming once a year. The man standing in the middle at the front of the group was Markus. He was in his early thirties and taller than his personal guards flanking him by a full head with a massive frame that put Tully's to shame. Short, dark brown hair was combed back from a broad face that lacked any emotion whatsoever, as though the proceedings held no more interest for him than drying paint.

He was the leader of the numerous districts in their territory and the one who set and enforced the laws by which they lived. His position was held by the strength of his will and fists and stories abounded of his cruel nature. Corin had only seen him twice before during his yearly rounds to those businesses that owed debts high enough to claim his attention. Scott's hotel had been on the list for the past two years. Though Corin had always tried to remain inconspicuous when the leader came by, Markus' calculating, hazel eyes had tracked his every movement until Corin would finally manage to slip out of sight.

"Take *him*!"

Corin wrenched his gaze away from Markus when the lobby fell into a tense silence. His mother was pointing a bony finger in his direction and staring from him to the leader and back again. A shadow of dread crept over him as Markus turned to look at him as well. The impassive expression on his chiseled features remained, even as his eyes heated with an indefinable emotion. Corin's mouth went dry and every muscle in his body locked into place.

"Take him," Doreen repeated. "He's a hard worker and trained to please. Men pay top dollar for him. The money we just gave you is all from his services last night. You'll earn back what we owe in only a month with him."

Corin could only stare at his mother, horrified and dumbstruck at her proposition. He knew she despised him, but to sell him into slavery... And to a man whose very reputation struck fear into the bravest of men in the outlying districts. They were all looking at him now—awaiting Markus' verdict with bated breath.

"All right then," Markus said in a deep bass. "This will square your debt to me, but watch yourself. If I have to visit this establishment one more time, I may not be satisfied with just one offering." His eyes alighted on Madeline and Doreen meaningfully, stating his message more clearly than words ever could.

The two men holding Scott released him instantly and started toward Corin. He wanted to run, to hide like a coward until this all blew over, but his body refused to obey. Finally, when one of the thugs grabbed his arm, he snapped out of his paralysis and tried to escape, but the men were faster. Each one took him by the arms and forced him out from behind the desk and over to the mountain of a man that now owned him.

Madeline ran out behind them in a breathless rush. "Mom, how could you do this? He's your son, not a slave!"

"No!" Amy, who'd been hiding in a niche behind the desk, ran around and struggled valiantly in her sister's arms when Madeline swept her up. "Cory!" Her little fists reached out, straining for her brother and grasping at empty air.

"He was *never* my son," Doreen said coldly. "He was born a slave, and he'll always be one."

Corin winced when the leader took his chin in hand and forced their gazes to meet. Markus towered well over a foot above him, his narrowed, implacable eyes boring down on him without mercy.

"You have one minute to say goodbye."

The man released his jaw, but he found himself immobilized again. Was this really happening? Would he be hauled away, never to see his sisters again? As he continued to gaze up into Markus' hard, uncaring face, he knew the answers. He'd waited too long to kill Scott or run with his sisters. Madeline had been right. He should have taken the initiative long ago, and now they would all pay for his hesitancy.

Nodding once, he turned when the thugs withdrew their hold and walked back to his sisters. Amy wriggled out of Madeline's arms and he knelt in time to welcome her charge. She buried her face in his neck and hugged him so tightly it pulled at his wounds, but he didn't care.

"Please don't go. You promised you would never leave."

Corin clutched her tiny frame and buried his face in her velvety curls. Her fresh, flowery scent seeped into his lungs and filled his head. "I'm sorry, baby girl. We'll see each other again soon, I promise."

Amy pulled back and sniffed softly. "But I love you."

His eyes stung with tears he refused to shed. This wasn't forever. He wouldn't let it be. "I love you too, sweetheart." With a kiss on her nose, he whispered, "Take care of your sister for me, 'kay?" When she nodded sullenly, he stood and looked to Madeline. She was a young woman, he realized belatedly, with chin held high and back straight with pride. When had he missed that leap of maturity, and what would happen to her once he was gone?

Madeline crossed to him slowly, pain etched in every beautifully pure feature. She stopped inches from him and Corin leaned down to place his forehead against hers. "Wait for me," she whispered. "I'll find you one day, no matter what."

Corin laughed gently at her theft of his role. He was the one who was supposed to be offering assurances, not the other way around. "I'm so proud of you. Keep looking behind your shoulder. I'll be there soon." He kissed her lips and remained there for several seconds as she captured his face in both hands then she let go and took a deliberate step back. Corin was about to turn when Scott took his arm above the elbow and yanked him close.

In a voice only the two of them could hear, he rasped, "Have fun. I know I will."

Corin followed the flick of his gaze to Madeline and felt a rage so strong it eclipsed all else. Before the man could react, he pulled his arm free, curled his fist and crashed it straight into the bridge of Scott's nose. In the next heartbeat, Corin was on him, driving him to the ground and pummeling his fists into his stepfather's face.

"You touch her and I'll kill you! You hear me! I'll tear you apart and make you beg for death!" Arms banded around his chest and lifted him easily, but he fought against the hold with a fury unleashed. "I'll kill you!" he screamed. "Let me go!" His feet flailed for purchase and only then did he realize that it was Markus who had him in his grip.

Scott jumped up from the floor and wiped at the blood pouring from his nose. He reared his fist to strike back, but it never reached Corin. Markus took the brunt of the punch in one hand and twisted savagely until Scott cried out and fell to his knees, fingers still caught in the larger man's fist.

"You ever raise a hand to my slave again and I'll kill you myself." He wrenched hard again, eliciting another strangled cry. "Understand?"

Scott nodded and collapsed when Markus released him.

The leader increased his hold on Corin and physically carried him out of the hotel, but Corin was too incensed to stop fighting. "You…" He kicked at Markus' shins, still glaring at Scott, "hurt her and I'll…" More struggling. "Let me go." As the front doors closed behind them, he twisted around and shouted, "I'll kill you!"

His energy was fading rapidly and the pain of his torn body was beginning to override the tide of his anger. There were two Hummers outside with three motorcycles behind them. Markus carried him to a huge, black Harley and dropped him ungracefully to the ground. The agony in Corin's gut brought him to his knees, or it would have had Markus not snaked out one arm and caught him. The pressure around his midsection caused his stomach to heave, but it was completely empty. Not even acid came up this time. When he was finished dry heaving, the leader tried to stand him up to no avail. Curling both arms around his aching stomach, Corin had no choice except to lean into Markus' firm body.

"What's wrong?"

Corin shook his head and bit out, "Nothing." When Markus turned him without warning and pressed the fingers of one hand into his lower abdomen, Corin shouted, though it came out more as a ragged, breathless wail.

"James, take my bike," Markus said above him. "We're going back to Carnasess. Parland, Terry, you're with me. The rest of you go with Tully to the last two businesses on the list and report to me tonight."

Humiliation at his weakness rose swiftly as Markus picked him up again and carried him to the nearest Hummer. The fire in his back, however, ended any protests he might have made. Once in the vehicle, he was situated on the leader's lap like a ragdoll and held against the corded muscles of Markus' wide chest. When the Hummer jolted to a start and bounced along the potholes marking the parking lot, he was too busy fighting off waves of nausea and pulsing cramps to concern himself with the blow to his ego at being held like a child.

A small whimper slipped past his compressed lips and he shrank involuntarily from Markus' large hand as it came up to his face. To his surprise, though, the man merely smoothed back the sweat-soaked tendrils of his hair and feathered a thumb lightly over his temple in a soothing rhythm as hot breath fanned across his closed lids. Eventually, the road evened out and Corin was lulled into the depths of his exhaustion by the rumbling vibrations of the vehicle and the steady beat of the leader's heart.

* * * *

Corin awoke to jostling and the clamor of voices raised in all manner of temperament. It was difficult at first. His mind didn't want to surface from the fog of decadent rest it was immersed in. The temptation to let it take the lead and pull him back under was arrested only by the unfamiliar assault to his senses that triggered a rise of alarm. Laughter, shouts, arguments and more seemed to come from all around him — and from men and women alike. Rich aromas of roasted meats, spices, cologne and scented candles competed with the mild undertones of sweat, animals and cigarette smoke.

And there was heat!

It permeated his skin and settled into his bones, the sensation so rare it stole his thoughts. Never had he been allowed a coat or even a sweater. Never been permitted a heater to warm the shed he slept in or given an adequate blanket for covering. The heat of the desert sun was sweltering and dry but this was different. Pleasant.

Corin shifted his body to stretch and found himself restricted. When he opened his eyes, it was to find a man's face staring down at him. The five o'clock shadow on his jaw gave him a brutal edge accentuated by dark, winged brows and high cheekbones. He was broodingly handsome in a way that added mystery to his dark appeal. It was his eyes, however, that cleared Corin's disorientation and brought his memories roaring back to life. The thugs. Doreen. His sisters. *His sisters!*

They were gone. *He* was gone. Sold as a slave to the most powerful, feared and hated man in the entire territory. Corin shoved hard at the chest glued to his side, but he was only drawn in tighter.

"Hold still," Markus said in a voice too low to be overheard by others.

A loud outburst from a crowd of people sitting around a circular table ahead of them made him start. He got his first real look at his surroundings and stared in wide-eyed wonder and, he had to admit, more than a little intimidation. They seemed to be in an enormously extensive one-story building held up by stone columns set periodically in all directions. Each one was uniquely stylized and thick enough for a man of Markus' size to easily hide behind. The floor was made of rough granite that had to span at least a hundred square yards and the people that traversed it were even more amazing.

He'd never seen such a diverse congregation of citizens from the many districts that made up the southwestern territory they were in. He'd never even left the hotel, for that matter, but many of the guests liked to talk, and he'd always listened when given the opportunity. For every compliment he'd heard from a person about their neighboring districts, he must have heard about ten complaints or insults. Though all of the districts were governed by the same laws and ultimately answerable to Markus, they each had their own elected delegate and way of living.

Countless brawls had occurred at the hotel between guests from different districts whose righteous anger usually boiled down to a simple conflict, one that could easily be solved if they dared to let their delegates take it to the leader. But then, Corin couldn't blame them for their reticence, not with the rumors he'd heard of the man. Murder, torture and plundering were only ripples in the lake of his repertoire.

As they headed toward the left side of the building, Corin took notice of the blatant stares they received from all those they passed. Or rather, that he was receiving. People of all ranks and origins stopped what they were doing to watch. Some turned the other way without a second glance while others glared openly with shrewd, dissecting eyes. Shame scalded his face and he struggled once more to break free then ceased when Markus growled menacingly.

"I can walk," Corin protested.

"No, you can't, and if you fight me one more time, I'll strip you down right here, lock a chain around your neck, and make you crawl on your hands and knees the rest of the way."

Corin paled at the bald threat reflected in the gleam in the leader's eyes. He darted his gaze back out over the crowds and noticed for the first time the slaves nearly hidden among the free people. They seemed to blend into the scenery for the most part, unseen and unheard. It wasn't hard to differentiate the working slaves from those meant for pleasure. All were clothed, unlike a few he'd seen at the hotel, but the pleasure slaves were less so and appeared almost nonexistent in their submissiveness.

Until their Masters got them alone in a bedroom, he was sure.

When they reached the far side, Markus nodded to two well-built men standing in front of a door, who opened it for him. Inside was a long, white tiled corridor with multiple, equally white doors on either side. The absolute silence in the wake of the pandemonium just on the other side of the door made his ears ring.

The change was so bizarre, he blurted out, "How?"

Markus turned immediately to his right and pressed a button to an elevator. He walked inside and from a panel of buttons ranging from basement level to ten, selected the top floor. "How what?"

"How is it we can't hear the people out there?"

The leader peered down at him with a look of consternation. "How old are you?"

"Twenty."

"And you've lived your whole life at that hotel?"

"Yeah," he replied, although he didn't know what that had to do with his question.

"Master."

"What?"

"You will address me as Master at all times. Failure to do so will result in punishment."

Corin fumed silently, not quite ready to take the first step that would signal the end of his freedom. Scott may have worked him like a slave, sold him like a slave, but Corin's reasons for obeying had been born of sacrifice and protection. Without Madeline and Amy to care for, his only motivation was to stay alive long enough to escape and find them.

The elevator doors opened and they entered a corridor nearly identical to the one they'd come from, only this was much shorter and had only a single door at the other end. Markus walked to this and spoke, "Hammond." A tiny light on a small panel about the size of Corin's palm flashed from red to green and the door slid noiselessly to the side.

The urge to inquire about that particular device warred with his stubbornness and, of course, the choice that would get him no answers won out. The room Markus walked into somewhat resembled an antique parlor he'd seen once in an old magazine. It formed a U shape with the front door at the curve. On an elevated platform directly ahead stood a white gloss grand piano with floor-to-ceiling bay windows beyond that. Standing and hanging plants of an assorted variety were interspersed with lamps that lent a relaxing ambiance with their soft light.

As the door slid closed behind them, Markus walked to the right and Corin gaped at the opulence spread out before him. The space was huge and completely open like the building next door with similar pillars, although they seemed to be in place more for decoration than practicality. His reflection shone in the polished wood flooring and the wood-paneled walls were decorated with sedate paintings and tapestries. There seemed to be every current source of leisure one could fit into an oversized apartment. A record player, casements of books, a pool table, even a Jacuzzi lined the walls along with many other things. At the far end stood a massive four-poster bed, which seemed to be Markus' destination.

Corin's breath came faster as they drew closer. He knew it was what Markus had traded his dues for, a slave that would cater to his every sexual whim, but after last night, he didn't think he could survive another round. While Markus was only one man, he was sure to have an appetite that would break Corin in his current condition. It was too soon, the pain still too bright in his memory and body. He scanned the area for any exit doors but found none. The front door had only admitted them with the sound of Markus' voice and, chances were, it would require the same to leave.

In a desperate bid for control, he tried to squelch the panic seizing his heart as the suffocating finality of his fate wormed its way past his barriers of fortitude. He would get through this, he would survive, and nothing would stop him from eventually escaping to find his sisters.

Chapter Four

The leader stopped several paces from the bed and slowly lowered Corin to his feet. This time, he was able to support himself with minimal discomfort. Markus continued to the bed and emptied the contents of his pockets onto a dark wood nightstand. "Take your clothes off," he ordered without turning around.

Corin glanced around again in futility. There was no way out.

Markus lifted one brow at him and when there was no response, sighed aggrievedly and walked around the bed to an ornate bureau on the other side large enough to accommodate four fully-sized men standing shoulder to shoulder. Like everything else in the penthouse, it reeked of affluence and the overindulgence of a man who had more money than he knew what to do with. Riches gained from the tyrannical extraction of the hard-earned dollar from working class people. How much food had this monster taken from the mouths of children just to feed his extravagance? How many people had become slaves for their inability to keep up with the increasing rate of rent?

Corin glared with undisguised malice until he saw the leather-bound switch Markus withdrew from the bureau and placed beside him on the foot of the bed where he sat down. "Your mother told me you were trained. Did she lie?"

Corin swallowed audibly. She hadn't lied. He recalled every lesson learned at the tail end of a whip, cane and any other instrument his stepfather had found at his disposal. Every humiliation and act of forced degradation. Maybe, if he hadn't been so recently and violently reminded of his place, he might have held onto his silent defiance. But the switch deflated it like so much hot air, and the man who threatened to wield it was no doubt well beyond Scott's caliber of sadism.

"No," he replied softly. With hands that shook only a little, he lifted the hem of his shirt then stopped. The wounds at the base of his spine had bled and dried, fusing the material to his broken skin. Bracing himself, he jerked hard. The shirt came up to the middle of his back where it snagged on the caked discharge of more welts. Corin took a moment to breathe through the stinging burn then tried again — and failed. He was about to attempt a third time when he heard Markus huff impatiently. The leader stood and closed the distance between them in two long strides. From a sheath strapped to his belt, he extracted a wickedly curved knife and brought it to Corin's chin.

"N-no, please!" Corin tripped over his own feet when he tried to get away, but Markus hauled him back by the arm.

"I'm not going to use this on you. Hold still."

Corin's entire body was shaking now, his eyes fixed to the ten-inch blade held so close he could almost feel its steel kiss. Markus let go of him then pulled on the collar of his shirt. Angling the tip of the blade down, he sliced through the cloth with frightening ease. When the two halves fell apart, the man paused then raised his free hand to the bite marks circling Corin's nipples. With a touch so light it almost tickled, Markus traced the dented outlines then ran the pads of his fingers over the bruises coloring protruding ribs.

"Turn around."

Corin obeyed without argument, his entire world narrowed down to the blade in the leader's hand and the pain it was *not* inflicting. The material at his back parted down the center and the strong band of Markus' arm reached around his chest. Without warning, the material on his left shoulder blade was ripped away. In one fluid movement, Markus switched arms and repeated the process to the right side. Corin's hands flew to the arm holding him as his sore flesh blazed anew. It wasn't until seconds later that he recognized the slight brush of the leader's hand tracing the edges of the reopened welts. Like before, the touch was shockingly gentle and more than a little unnerving.

Markus pulled his arm away and set the blade to the rear of Corin's pants. There was more tearing as the jeans were ripped from the wounds on the backs of his thighs and tugged down to his ankles. Once more, fingers glided over his skin to take stock of the evidence of his abuse. Markus didn't stop there. He pried open the mounds of Corin's ass to inspect his vulnerable entrance then shuffled around to handle his bruised cock and balls, lifting and turning them until Corin whimpered and flinched reflexively. Markus looked up then, and the black fire burning from his eyes caused a shiver to course down Corin's spine.

The leader rose swiftly and strode toward the nightstand. On a square, metal plate affixed to the wall above it, he pushed and held down a button. "Heather, have Spencer come to my quarters with his bag immediately."

"Yes, Master," a female answered.

Corin watched warily as Markus sheathed his knife then opened a door he hadn't seen before next to the head of the bed, entering what looked to be a bathroom. He brought out two white towels and spread them out over the black silk comforter on the bed then went back to the bathroom for a small garbage bag. This he handed to Corin and ordered him to fill it with his ruined clothes and shoes. With that done, Markus took the bag and pointed to the bed.

"Lie down on the towels."

The leader didn't wait to make sure he obeyed, instead withdrawing to the other side of the penthouse. Corin forced his feet to move and climbed onto the decadent bed. When he was standing, it came to the tops of his thighs and practically enveloped him in its enormity. It was larger than any he'd ever seen— larger even than the shed he'd been relegated to since his toddler years at the hotel.

He hesitated briefly, unsure of which position to assume on the towels, as Markus hadn't specified how he wanted his slave to lie. His stepfather's words rang with humbling clarity through his mind, "*A good slave always makes its body available to its Master. It will expose itself for the Master's view and use at all times.*" If Corin had been back in one of the rooms at the hotel with Scott looming over him, he would have his ass in the air with limbs tucked underneath. But it wasn't Scott who held dominion over his body anymore, and he was definitely not in a ramshackle room with stained sheets under his knees. Finally, he settled on lying flat on his belly, head turned to stare at the switch that would probably be introduced to his backside before the night was over.

A few minutes later, the front door opened and Markus returned with a man at his side. The stranger, who must have been the man called Spencer, was much shorter and balding with a generous gut that had likely never missed a meal. Corin's eyes widened at the sight of the black leather satchel in his hand, sure that whatever it contained was meant for him.

"I need you to take a look at him," Markus said to the squat man. "I think he might have internal damage, as well as the cuts on his backside." They neared the bed and Markus stood aside while Spencer placed his satchel on the bed next to Corin. The stranger began poking and prodding at the welts on Corin's shoulders, lower back and thighs, causing him to wince and grapple the blanket in his fists.

"I'll need a washcloth and a large bowl of warm water," Spencer said with gruff authority.

To Corin's amazement, Markus complied without a hint of indignation, as if it were nothing for the stranger to order him about like a common servant. The leader came back shortly and pulled a lamp table to the bed where he set down the supplies. Corin gritted his teeth, burying his face in the crook of one arm as Spencer proceeded to wipe down his ravaged skin in unsympathetic, brisk strokes.

"None of these appears to be infected or needs stitches," Spencer commented in an uninterested tone. "I'll give you some ointment before I leave that should minimize the scarring." He tapped Corin on the hip and said, "Turn over. Put your head toward the headboard."

Corin did as he was told, clenching his fists at his sides to keep from hiding his exposed cock. It was ludicrous to think that this was in any way different from servicing the men his stepfather had sold him to, yet somehow, he found it harder to assume submission and distance himself, and not simply because of his fear of the leader and the toys in the black bag. At the hotel, he'd always known that no matter how bad the episodes got, they would end eventually. He could take refuge in honest work and the love of his sisters in between his carnal duties, but there would be none of that here. His life would now consist only of satiating the appetite of a man he despised only slightly less than Scott and whoever else he shared him with.

Staring at the ceiling, he held his breath as Spencer inspected his balls and cock with a touch that was harsh in comparison to Markus'. He squeezed the tip and pried open the slit then moved up to push his fingers onto several areas of Corin's abdomen. The entire area was sore and when the man applied pressure on one particular spot, it evoked a sharp cramp that caused Corin to jerk and hiss.

"Does that hurt?" Spencer asked.

Corin frowned up at the man. Of course it hurt, but what did a free man care for the pain of a slave? Perhaps Markus was trying to assess the extent of the damage to his newly acquired property, deciding whether he was worth keeping. If that was the case, however, why hadn't he done that before agreeing to take him?

Corin looked to the leader who nodded his head. "Yes," he whispered.

Spencer continued upward and Corin was unable to hold back a gasp as fingers jabbed into his tender stomach. "How often were you fed, boy?"

Fed, not how often he ate. It grated on his nerves that Spencer so readily assumed he'd been a slave before Markus had taken him, even though the man was not far off the mark. Corin thought about the question then answered, "I eat about every other day."

"What were you given?"

"I made soup for myself," he lied defiantly. They didn't need to know that it had been Madeline who'd secretly given him food whenever he'd starved from punishment or neglect.

"Where did you get this one?" Spencer asked with a cursory glance over his shoulder at the leader.

"A hotel on the border of the territory. His father owns it and was renting him out."

"He is *not* my father," Corin interjected with vehemence. Not the smartest thing to do, but both men ignored him, regardless.

Spencer tapped him again and ordered, "Lift your knees."

The man rifled through his bag and began removing several odd-looking objects from it. When Corin saw a long instrument made of polished metal and a needle with three vials, his panic renewed itself and he tried to scramble from the bed. Markus was on him instantly and pushed him down, trapping his wrists above his head in one hand while leaning on his chest with the other, but still Corin fought, his fear lending him false courage.

"Enough," Markus said in a quiet tone—inflectionless, calm and collected as ever.

Corin's eyes flew to the hilt of the knife at the leader's belt and it took all that he had to cease his struggles, his breath coming in rapid pants as Spencer pushed his heels to the backs of his thighs. His legs were spread wide and he heard Spencer grumble, "He's probably never had an examination before. Just try to hold him still."

When the cold, unyielding tip of the metal instrument came into contact with his entrance, his lungs heaved with air they couldn't seem to drag in and he trembled with the effort to hold still.

"Relax." Spencer slapped Corin's inner thigh, but that did nothing to help the situation. With a sigh, he said, "You'll have to calm him down. If he keeps this up, I'll end up doing more harm than good."

Markus angled himself so that his face was directly above Corin's. "Who trained you, Cory?"

"C-Corin," he corrected again thoughtlessly.

"Corin, answer my question."

Confusion at the inquiry somehow managed to break through his anxiety and distract him from the cool, metal tip still pressed to his tender channel. "Scott."

"If he trained you, then why do you resist me?"

Corin shook his head, brow furrowing at the line of questioning. "Because I'm not... I wasn't a slave then. It was different."

The older man nodded then as though he understood. "I see. So, you offered your services willingly."

"No!"

"Fear, then?"

Corin sucked in a breath as the instrument was swiftly inserted. The film of lubrication that coated it didn't ease the surge of pain that rippled through him, causing his skin to break out into a clammy sweat.

"Your sisters," Markus said in revelation. "You obeyed your stepfather to protect them."

Too focused on keeping his stomach from trying to produce more vomit, he only nodded with a twinge of irritation at the man's astuteness.

"Perhaps I should've taken them as well."

His better judgment fled on the wings of anger and he renewed his struggles with vigor. "If you hurt them, I'll kill you, too!" Corin realized his mistake as soon as the words were out. A threat from a slave on its Master's life was grounds for a death penalty. At the hotel, he'd seen slaves beaten and mutilated for far less.

Spencer withdrew the object from Corin's anus and straightened with a shocked expression. "I'll come back later."

"Finish your examination, Doc," Markus said. "It's getting late." The strange expression and slight smile that lifted one corner of his mouth were so unexpected that they threw Corin off balance.

"I'm pretty much done here, anyways. Whatever was used on him created an anal fissure that's become infected. He won't be ready for full use for at least two weeks." Spencer went on with his analysis as he took a small, clear bottle from his bag and, flipping it upside down, pushed a syringe into its top and pulled the plunger down.

"From the discoloration of his stool, I'd say he probably has an ulcer as well, if not several. They're usually caused by a certain type of bacteria and easily taken care of, but it appears as if extreme malnourishment and stress have made them worse. Good news is I don't think they're ruptured. I'll give Heather some antibiotic pills to bring to you. Make sure he takes them every morning and night on a full stomach. He'll also need to be placed on a very strict diet. No greasy or acidic foods. I'll forward the details to Heather."

He rolled Corin's hip to the side and jammed the needle into the fat of his buttock. Using another needle attached to a long, thin tube, he filled the three vials with blood from Corin's arm and wrote on them with a black marker. "I'll check him for diseases and have the results back to you soon." After returning his instruments to his satchel, he sent Corin one last scrutinizing stare. "You'll need to retrain him. I still have the shock collar I used on my slave."

"That won't be necessary," Markus said as he released Corin's wrists and stood. "I'll take care of it."

Spencer grunted and handed him a blue jar. "Apply this to his backside twice a day. If you have any questions, call me."

"Thanks, Doc." Markus walked the other man out then came back some time later with a bowl of mixed fruit. Pointing at his feet, he said, "Kneel."

When Corin obeyed, keeping his eyes downcast, in part to hide the animosity behind them, Markus set the plate down on the floor in front of him.

"Eat." Without another word, the leader retreated to the bathroom where the sound of running water filled the silence.

The temptation to fling the bowl at the wall was almost too great to suppress. Being treated like a dog produced a whole new level of humility that should've been impossible, considering everything he'd already been through. Maria, the slave Doreen rented during the busy season at the hotel, had once told him that it was not a collar or brand that made a slave, but the abandonment of pride and hope. At the time, he'd been recovering from a brutal session with Scott and one of his drinking buddies and had felt like giving up. He'd hated her for the insinuation that he was no more a free person than she was, but had come to realize later just what her words meant.

They gave him comfort now. No matter what Markus tried to make him, he would always be his own man in his heart.

Unable to resist the lure of food, he ate as much as his stomach could handle. Markus came out in a cloud of steam with an open terry cloth robe partially covering his body. Corin tried unsuccessfully not to stare at the naked physique that was revealed. Hard lines spanned out from a torso that was almost as broad as it was long and covered in a fine smattering of dark hairs. Markus' legs were as thick as telephone poles and the cock that dangled between them…

Even soft as it was, Corin knew it would tear him open if he weren't properly prepared, and nothing about the man's demeanor gave him the impression that such care would take place. The leader pursed his lips at the remnants of the meal, but merely told him to get back on the bed. From a drawer at the base of the bureau, he took out a pair of black leather cuffs and bound them to Corin's wrists.

"Wait. I have to go to the bathroom." His statement went ignored as the leader rolled him onto his front and started applying the cream Spencer had supplied onto his wounds.

"You will speak only when spoken to," Markus began in his deep, imperious voice. "If you have a question, you may look up to my chin. Otherwise, your eyes will stay on the ground. Whenever you're with me, you will kneel at my feet or walk two paces behind me. When I'm gone, you will clean my quarters exceptionally. Any dereliction of your duties will result in punishment. Am I clear?"

Corin stubbornly held his tongue, foolish as it was considering that he already had a punishment coming to him for threatening the leader's life and making things worse wasn't exactly in his best interest. His mind was still trying to wrap itself around Markus' commands. It was hard to fathom that the simple liberties he'd had just earlier that day were so inexorably gone now—that he was reduced to the status of a creature whose only goal was to please its Master day and night.

When Markus had finished his ministrations, he put the jar onto the top shelf of the nightstand. The chain linking the cuffs together was separated then reattached behind one of the bars of the headboard so that Corin's wrists were pulled above his head once again. The leader tucked the top sheet and comforter over his body before walking back to the other side of the penthouse.

Corin waited with tense expectation of what was to come next, but there was nothing. The medication on his lacerations leached the heat from them and numbed his skin as the warmth of the blanket soaked into his bones. Despite the cuffs, the feel of so much luxury was like a siren drawing him down into the depths of opulence. It was so peaceful he'd have fallen to the exhaustion that tugged at his consciousness if not for the tingling in his bladder that quickly became a burning demand.

After some time, there was a low hum of voices and he recognized Tully's rough baritone, but the visitors remained out of his sight. An hour or two passed before Markus finally came back to the bed. By that time, Corin's bladder was screaming at him and he could no longer put off the inevitable. He stared at Markus' chin as the man approached and was noticed immediately. *Thank God!*

"Speak."

"May I go to the bathroom...Master?" he tagged on at the last second.

The hint of something indecipherable played across the other man's lips and was gone in the next moment. Markus removed the cuffs and tilted his head in the direction of the bathroom. Corin jumped up and paused briefly to gawp at the next room before entering it. Everything was pristine white, except for the beige marble countertops, stainless steel faucets, and shower stall trim. A bathtub at least half as big as the Jacuzzi lay to his left and on the opposite wall above the sink spanned a tall, wood-framed mirror.

The toilet on the far side beckoned and he hurried over to relieve himself. Markus was waiting for him afterwards and reattached the cuffs before nudging him onto the mattress. Corin raised his hands, expecting to be locked into place again, but the leader only lay down and tugged him forward, so he was sprawled on top of the man's lower half. There was enough give in the chain linking the cuffs to allow him to rest his head on his hands below Markus' ribcage. The man's large hand threaded through his hair and his sides were trapped between two longs legs while Markus' substantial cock, at half-mast now, dug into his belly.

As the covers were pulled up to his head and tucked in around him, he listened to the sounds of the leader's breathing even out, praying this would finally be the end of his long day. And it was.

Chapter Five

Fingers gently massaged Corin's scalp, feathered over his nose and cheeks, and traced the seam of his lips. The touch was soft, soothing and completely incongruous with what he was accustomed to waking up to. Corin opened his eyes and tried in vain to move. The strong scents of musk and soap brought him around to full awareness and he looked up. Markus' brown eyes met his, so dark with lust they appeared black in the dim light of dawn seeping through the cream-colored gauze covering the windows. Alarm needled its way into his heart when the leader pushed on his shoulders, forcing him to scoot down until a large cock sprang up in front of his face. It was hard with morning urgency and already so engorged that veins bulged along its thick length.

He knew what to do without asking and kept his gaze down to hide the contempt he was sure was written all over his face. When he gripped the cock in both hands, Markus braced the sides of Corin's head, brushing his hair back so he could get a clear view of the show. Corin wanted to rush through it so that he could get his first degradation of the day over with, but his training kicked in. Scott had taught him all the tricks—now he just had to find the ones that worked for Markus.

He started with the tip, rolling his tongue around the circumcised head and dipping into the weeping slit. The taste was slightly salty but clean, nothing like most of the unwashed patrons he'd had to service. Tucking his knees beneath him to get a better angle, he enclosed the head in his mouth and sucked down until it touched the back of his throat. This pulled a groan from the leader and Corin repeated the action, pumping one hand at the base. With his other, he fondled Markus' balls, pressing his fingers to the perineum and massaging it.

Marcus began swiveling his hips, forcing more and more of his straining erection into the throat constricting it. Corin took his cues from the man's soft moans, his hitched breaths and the insistence of his fists in Corin's hair. Legs bent at the knees squeezed his sides, keeping him in place. He'd always wondered what it was about blow jobs that was so great that men would pay, hurt or steal another person's will to get them. He'd never had anyone touch his cock for more than the deliverance of pain, never felt it embedded in the heat of another's mouth or welcoming entrance. His only experience had been with his own hand, and that was only ever to relieve the pressure once it built to a certain level.

Sex, for him, was no more than the endurance of agony brought on by people who took it as their monetary right. Not even the women he'd pleasured with his mouth and fingers while their husbands watched or took him from behind had ever shown kindness, and why should they? He'd been a slave in their paid rooms, just as much as he was a slave to the man using him now.

Markus' groans quickly turned to low grunts, letting Corin know he was getting close. All of a sudden, the man pushed Corin's hands away and began thrusting his hips vigorously. Corin opened up just in time to accept the full length barreling past his natural resistance and stretching his throat unbelievably wide. Each powerful buck filled him with more than he thought he could take. With one last thrust, hot spurts of semen shot into his belly while his face was held in a strong grip against Markus' groin. The body underneath him shook until he'd swallowed every drop of cum. When he was finally released, he stayed where he was, head bent and arms tucked in to await his next order.

Markus unfastened the cuffs and threw them to the side, leading Corin into the bathroom afterwards and relieving himself at the toilet. He motioned for Corin to do the same and turned on the shower when he was done. After pulling Corin in with him, the leader picked up a bottle and loofa and began washing himself. Inside were five showerheads, two on each side and one in front high enough to spray down onto Markus' head. The stall was huge, with plenty of room for Corin to keep his distance, which he did. From the opposite end, he took in the variety of bottled soaps that appeared so expensive, he was afraid to touch them.

Markus solved that problem a few minutes later.

The leader took a washcloth from one of the hanging shelves and poured onto it the same soap he'd used on himself. With that, he washed every inch of Corin's body. It was unsettling to say the least, and when Markus turned him around, he gasped and palmed the wall in front of him to keep his balance. The man had a slick finger at his hole and was slowly pushing it inside. The intrusion was more uncomfortable than painful as the first knuckle slipped in, but it was the thought of what else would be inserted in there that had him so tense he could barely breathe.

Warmth bathed his backside as Markus moved close and reached around with his other hand to gently clean Corin's flaccid cock and balls. They stayed that way for some time, the leader in no hurry to finish playing with his slave — then it was over. Corin stood motionless and watched from the peripheral of his vision as Markus washed his hair thoroughly then rinsed it clean, along with his body.

He was towel dried after Markus had taken care of himself then given a toothbrush, shaving cream and a razor to use. The leader also started on his own hygiene, gesturing for Corin to lie on the bed after they were done, and applying more cream to his wounds. When the ministrations were complete, Markus dressed in jeans, boots and a form-fitting T-shirt then outfitted himself with a harness that held a gun along one side of his ribs and a belt that held his knife.

"Come," he ordered.

Corin obediently followed him to the other side of the penthouse. Whereas on the bedside, wood had been the predominant component of the furniture, here were sleek lines and shining metal surfaces. The black glass-top table set close to the center could easily seat eight people and a half-bar separated a large kitchen full of appliances he couldn't even begin to name. Pictures on the walls depicted scenes of nature and animals, but a few were of people. They seemed to greatly resemble Markus, particularly a man with the same coloring and height. Corin assumed it was the leader's father and wondered what the man must think of his son now.

There was a sharp rap on the door and a woman who looked to be in her late twenties let herself in. She had straight, dirty blonde hair held back in a single braid that fell to her slim hips and a face that would have been plain had it not been for its lively animation. She appeared to be high-spirited by the way she smiled openly and bounced more than walked. A collar around her neck and a brand on the back of one her hands signified her slave status, but unlike most of the slaves Corin had met, she seemed to be happy.

"Sorry I'm late, Master," she said, placing several bags on the countertop next to the sink. "Doc stopped me at the last minute and asked me to give this to you." After handing one of the bags to Markus, she pulled out a folded piece of paper from her pants pocket. "He also gave me a list of foods to cook for your new slave so I had to run back and get some of the items. I'll bring the rest by later. Oh, is this him?"

The woman's bright blue eyes lit on him and Corin suddenly remembered his nudity. He cupped himself in embarrassment and started to back away, only to be halted by a sharp order from Markus.

"You will not move unless I tell you to," the leader said, his quiet voice no less commanding than a yell. Corin blushed furiously as his hands were pushed back to his sides and he was left standing in the middle of the area. The woman winked at him, which merely served to increase his humiliation.

"Doc said you'll find the antibiotics and everything you might need to train your new boy in there and to let him know if there's anything else you'd like."

"Thanks, Heather." Markus emptied the contents of his bag onto the table and sorted through them. Corin was absently surprised that the man didn't already have all of those things at his disposal. Among the items was another pair of cuffs of a similar fashion to the ones he'd worn last night, which the leader immediately secured to Corin's wrists and attached behind his back. He then took a thin, silver collar made of a light metal and locked it around Corin's neck with an Allen wrench smaller than a pen cap. From a casement off to the side, he grabbed a book and sat down at the head of the table. Without looking up, he pointed to the floor beside him and Corin shook with anger as he knelt at the leader's feet. The only consolation was that his back was now turned to the woman in the kitchen.

Soon, the delicious smells of eggs, bacon and more wafted through the air and Corin's stomach rumbled in anticipation. Though he'd eaten his fill last night, it had been close to four days before then that he'd had a halfway decent meal and been able to keep it down. He wouldn't even mind eating from the floor again if it meant appeasing his hunger pangs. The woman, Heather, set two plates in front of Markus and two mugs beside them, one with a straw.

Markus took several bites from one dish, put his fork down then brought a bagel to Corin's lips from the other dish. Corin glared in outright indignation. When the older man shrugged and moved to replace it, survival instincts prevailed over pride and he opened his mouth to accept the bite Markus fed him. The leader repeated the process of feeding them both in turns until half of the bagel was gone. He took out a pill from a bottle he'd set aside earlier and put it into Corin's mouth. Next came the mug with the straw and

Corin swallowed the pill, drinking half of the milk with a frown afterwards. It wasn't nearly as appealing as the strong coffee he was used to. When Markus brought more food to his lips, Corin shook his head and stared at the man's chin.

"Speak."

"Can I get a cup of coffee, Master?"

"No," Markus said firmly. "The caffeine will upset your ulcers. You will not ask me again for food or drinks. I'll decide what you can and can't have."

Anger surged again and before he could think twice, he ground out, "I'm not a dog. You can't just strip me of my rights and expect me to roll over and take it. All I want is a fucking cup of coffee!" Somewhere in the back of his mind, he knew his outburst had been building to the point of inevitability. He'd been sold by his mother, taken from the only two beings in the world that made his life worthwhile and thrust into the hands of a cruel authoritarian. He felt utterly lost and had reached his breaking point, but his momentum quickly fizzled under the hard glare of the man before him. It was measured, calculating and somehow more frightening than the brash rage of his stepfather's.

Markus stood, took an object from the table and hauled Corin over to the center of the room. He stuffed the object into his back pocket then banded one arm around Corin's waist in an unbreakable hold. Corin started to tremble and looked down at the knife strapped to the leader's belt, recalling the ease with which it'd sliced through his clothes the night before. With a gasp, he felt his cock taken into a solid grasp and pumped earnestly. To his stark horror, his body responded instantly. The pain of his welts and bruises flared excruciatingly at first, then seemed to blend with a wave of pleasure he was powerless to prevent. Blood pooled to his groin so fast it left him breathless and his member filled and lengthened despite his efforts to will it back down.

Corin struggled to get away, alarmed by the combination of the man's unyielding strength and the shock of the sensations coursing through his body. The hand was relentless as it fisted him in brisk, sure strokes, milking an arousal that sped well beyond Corin's control to stop. Heat swept through him at the humiliation and he turned his head against Markus' chest to cover the tears burning in his eyes. The knowledge that Heather was a silent witness somewhere in the background made his disgrace complete. There was no way she could miss the obvious sign of the physical enjoyment of his punishment.

His knees went weak and a soft whimper escaped as his balls tightened and fire raced down his spine. His orgasm was coming swiftly, but the hand abruptly stilled and squeezed just under the tip of his pulsing cock. He moaned at the jolt of renewed pain on his sensitive flesh as his release was suspended and material wrapped around the base of his member. Forced to lean into Markus' chest to keep from losing his balance when the man let go, he watched as a leather cock ring was strapped to his base and another strip was circled around his aching testes to pull them away from his groin.

Markus walked casually back to the table, only to return with several more items. He attached a spreader bar to Corin's legs just above his knees then pushed him down to a kneeling position. Corin was forced to display his jutting cock while the leader snapped on a leash to the back of his collar, looped it around the chain linking the wrist cuffs together and tied it off. A bandana was placed over his eyes and bound at the back of his head. He was panting and flinched involuntarily when a strip of duct tape sealed his mouth shut.

Helpless, mute and blind, the tears Corin had been holding in leaked out onto the cloth covering his face. It was all he could do to keep the whirlwind of his tangled emotions at bay. He'd never been punished like this and honestly didn't know if he'd rather be beaten. Fingers lightly brushed over his cheeks and neck, lingering at his throat then traveling down the expanse of Corin's chest to the patch of hair at his groin.

"You will learn to obey me, boy," Markus said softly, his face so close Corin could feel the hot puffs of his breath. "I am not a harsh Master, but this will continue until you've learned your place."

Corin shivered as the man's hands played over his skin for a few more minutes then drew away. There were words passed between Markus and Heather then the sound of the front door opening and closing. He lowered his ass to the floor, back straight to keep the collar from choking him, and tried to find a comfortable position.

"Wow," Heather piped up from the direction of the kitchen. "Doc told me you were barely trained, but I didn't think it was *that* bad. You're really lucky to have the leader for your Master, you know. Most other Masters would have beaten you senseless for that offense. You'll come to realize he's actually a fair man, though I'm sure right now you probably think a little less of him." Heather laughed lightheartedly. "I've never seen that man cause an ounce of pain that wasn't deserved. Even to his enemy."

Corin simply listened, too spent from his debasement to summon the snort of derision he might have made at her words otherwise.

"As slaves, there are certain rules we must adhere to," Heather rattled on. "As *his* slave, you'll have even more rules. He's got to keep face in front of his men if they're to follow him and give their lives to protect him. Having an errant boy like you defying his control, would lower his reputation and might give others the idea that they could replace him. If that happened, we'd all be in trouble. It's why he's never owned anyone before. Frankly, I'm surprised he bought you. Not that you aren't cute or anything—I can definitely see the attraction—but you're still a risk he doesn't need. Especially now."

A sliver of curiosity broke through the fog of Corin's misery. What could be going on now that made this period of Markus' rule more crucial than before? He knew there were a great number of people upset about some of the laws he'd implemented, but there had been no talk of an uprising.

There was another knock at the door and it opened at a voice command from Heather. "Hi, Josh. Did you bring the supplies I need?"

A man that sounded to be close to Heather's age answered, though his tone was much more sedate. "Yes, ma'am, and I got the candles you wanted."

"Excellent. They're Master's favorite. He'll be very pleased."

"Who's that?"

"Master's new slave. He still needs a lot of training, but I think he'll be a keeper." After a pause, she said, "Oh, Josh, calm down. You were never Master's boy, just a slave he took to his bed on occasion. Don't mind him, Corin. He's just jealous, although I can't see why.

He was elevated to a working slave a few months ago, which is definitely a step up from being a pleasure slave—at least when you have a Master like most of the jerks out there. Well, since you'll be taking care of the Master once you know all of the rules, I'll start explaining your duties around here."

The woman went on to describe the daily and weekly chores he would be required to do around the penthouse. There weren't necessarily a lot of things to clean, but apparently, Markus was an extremely meticulous man and liked his belongings cared for in a particular way. The melodic drone of Heather's voice helped to soothe some of his tension, though the pressure on his cock became increasingly uncomfortable. The whir of a vacuum cleaner filled his ears and a few minutes later, Josh's voice sounded so close he jerked, startled.

"He'll get tired of you soon and come back to me. Just wait." Then Josh moved away to finish his vacuuming.

Corin was so amazed at the man's audacity that it took a moment for it to register. Did Josh seriously think he wanted to be there, trussed up like a recalcitrant possession and stripped of all dignity? He burned with the urge to scream out, *You can have him, you ignorant fool!* Many times he'd wished this on Scott and all of the men who'd taken him cruelly, but to have a fellow slave think that this was desirable made his skin crawl.

It wasn't until hours later that the door opened again and he heard Markus' familiar voice. He listened to the leader greet the other two slaves then crouch in front of him. The cock ring was removed and he grimaced when a hand touched his swollen cock, but it was gentle this time, massaging at a slow pace and working at the congestion of blood until the discomfort finally faded. The bandana was next, as well as the leash and tape at his mouth. When Markus helped him to stand, he almost toppled over and had to steady himself against the leader's body. The spreader bar came off, followed by the cuffs, and Corin was so relieved that he almost thanked the leader.

Almost.

"You may use the bathroom," Markus said, as he collected the instruments and put them back on the table.

Corin took off without a word. Just as he was about to close the door for privacy, he heard Markus call out, "Leave it open."

Growling quietly in frustration, he went to the toilet and winced at the effort it took to relieve himself. By the time he was done, cramps had stolen his appetite and he wanted nothing more than to lie down but didn't think the leader would allow him that.

He found Markus sitting at the table again with more food in front of him. At the man's indication, he walked over and turned around, giving no resistance while his wrists were bound behind his back and he was signaled to kneel. He swallowed the first few bites of fruit salad with difficulty until his hunger kicked in and he eagerly finished the rest his food. When everything was gone, Markus pushed the plates away and dropped his hand to Corin's head. He caressed his hair lazily and slid his fingers repeatedly from the roots to the tips as though relishing its texture.

After a while, Markus stood and walked him to the center of the room. He placed one arm around Corin as before and clasped his limp cock. Corin groaned and clenched his eyes shut as another bout of shame heated his skin. He was handled with more care this time, the strokes not so much jerks as long pulls that enticed blood to pool at his base and fill his growing erection. Arousal rose swiftly, nearly catching him by surprise as his body gave into the will of its Master.

He might have taken true pleasure in this once. For countless nights he'd dreamt of a man that might touch him like this—bring him to the point of rapture until he begged for mercy then tipped him over the edge. Hold him tight through the throes of his release and whisper kind words as he floated back down. It had been a fantasy that had seen him through the worst of his abuse, one that was gone now and left him with only despair and the betrayal of his own body.

Markus picked up the pace of his hand, spreading fire down the length of Corin's engorged cock and making him pant with urgency. With a shadow of panic, he glanced down at the bulge in the leader's crotch revealing Markus' own arousal, and couldn't help the thrusting of his hips as his orgasm built like an imminent, crashing wave. Even after his member was squeezed just below the head and his climax was rebuffed, his pelvis rocked of its own accord, as if it could somehow regain what had been denied.

Markus trapped his erection in the cock ring then took his time affixing the rest of the instruments to Corin's body, smoothing over trembling flesh with his hands and leaning in close enough to warm Corin with his heat. The actions were almost tender and somehow left him bereft and confused when the man exited the apartment again. Heather and Josh also vacated the penthouse shortly thereafter, claiming they were done for the day.

"He usually has supper with his men," Heather was saying, "so he probably won't be back until late. I've put a plate of food for you in the fridge with a note for him so he can feed you when he returns." She patted his head in a gesture he assumed was meant to console. "It'll get better. Fighting him will get you nowhere. Trust me on this. I'll see you again tomorrow."

And with that, they were gone.

Corin tested the strength of his bonds and, after finding them as secure as before, bowed his head as far as the leash would let him. The grandfather clock standing against the front wall near the piano ticked away the seconds of his despondency. As the minutes turned to hours, his muscles began to cramp from the tight restriction. He longed to stretch out his legs, but didn't dare, for fear of being discovered. Although Markus had yet to hit him or even show a hint of anger, he didn't want to give the man any reasons to, or to think of new and humiliating punishments to inflict.

To keep his mind from the drastic turn of his life, he thought of his sisters and what they must be doing at that moment. Madeline was most likely finishing up with the housekeeping, grousing about the disturbing habits of the guests and the messes they left behind. Soon, she would be relieving Scott or Doreen at the front desk and sneaking into the back office once she was alone. With the busy season close to an end, she would have more time to focus on her art. She'd always been a gifted painter, even when she was little.

Corin almost smiled when he recalled the edible pictures she would make with her food as he tried to convince her to eat it. At age five, he'd been given the responsibility of caring for her immediately after birth so that Doreen could go back to work and sleep at night. It had been overwhelming at first, his only instructions given in a five minute lecture about formula measurements and diapers. The colic, constant feedings and changings on top of his long list of daily chores had been exhausting and earned him a lot of beatings when he couldn't keep up, yet it had been one of the happiest times in his life.

Doreen had allowed him to sleep in Madeline's room instead of the shed and there, he'd learned what it was like to be loved unconditionally, without pain and criticisms and harsh expectations. When Madeline had been old enough to draw with crayons, he had formulated stories from her pictures, putting into words the beauty of her imagination. That had all come to a stop, however, when Madeline had turned six. Doreen had decided she was old enough to help out with more than just the cooking and Scott had found other ways to put Corin to use.

Then Amy had been born. He'd once again been assigned to care for the youngest so everyone else could get their rest and have time for other things. His youngest sister had been twice the handful, though Amy had a way about her that made it all worthwhile. She'd loved to push his limits, but he'd never found them with her, even when many of her antics had gotten him into trouble. She was energetic and wild in many ways that were utterly endearing.

Corin hadn't been able to spend as much time with her as he had Madeline, not with Scott continually taking him away to sell him to others, but that hadn't lessened the bond of their relationship. Nor had Doreen's spiteful jealousy whenever her daughters had voiced their preference to play with him rather than her.

Were Amy and Madeline still safe without him there to distract their father? Scott's many threats rang through his mind, leaving little hope the man wouldn't stoop so low as to sell his own flesh and blood. Though Doreen loved her girls, she wasn't around all of the time, and she definitely wasn't strong enough to protect them.

Corin tensed when the front door opened. The scents of sweat and cigarette smoke reached his nose as he listened to heavy boots travel to the kitchen. There was some clattering then the sounds of a microwave running. After a sharp beep, the boots came toward him. The faint smell of Markus' aftershave wafted over him just before the leader gripped his stiff member. With aching relief, his cock was released and massaged until it no longer protruded from his groin with painful rigidity. Corin winced at the cramps in his muscles and stomach as he was raised and stripped of the rest of his bindings. Now that he could see again, he noticed the leader was damp with a fine sheen, as though he'd been working out. His breath smelled of spiced meats, which meant the smoke clinging to his clothes must've been second hand.

"Do you need to use the bathroom?" When Corin shook his head, he turned to pick up a bowl of what appeared to be stew and a cup.

Corin watched the man walk around to the other side of the penthouse, unsure of what to do and reluctant to move without permission.

"Come," Markus barked.

He rushed over to where the leader sat down in a large, brown recliner with an end table beside it. At a gesture, he knelt between Markus' legs and remained silent as he was fed. The stew was better than any he'd ever tasted, the beef chunks nearly melting in his mouth and there was so much, he couldn't finish it all. From beneath his lashes, he glanced up several times and saw Markus peering down at him with an inscrutable expression. Finally, Corin was given another pill to swallow and the dishes were set aside. The leader picked up a wide binder and placed it on the arm of the chair so he could review the contents of the papers inside. With a hand at the back of Corin's skull, he guided his head down to rest on one massive thigh.

Corin shifted uncomfortably, not sure of where to place his hands now that they were free and expecting at any moment to be pulled to the jeaned cock mere inches from his face. When nothing else happened, he willed the tension from his sore muscles and tried not to dwell on the intimacy of his position. It was odd being so close to what he'd been bought to appease without being forced to do anything. No one had ever wanted to touch him without demanding immediate attention. The absent caress of Markus' fingers threading through his hair lulled him into a light doze until the deep timbre of the man's voice startled him awake.

"What were the people like, the guests who stayed at your stepfather's hotel?"

"What?" Corin glanced up in bewilderment, narrowly remembering to avert his gaze to the lap in front of him when he saw the man's lips thin in displeasure. "Master," he tagged on. "What do you mean?"

"I've seen you work the front desk there before. Surely you spoke with some of the guests. What did they have to say?"

He opened and closed his mouth a few times, at a loss as to how to answer such a general question. "I don't know. Some talked about why they were traveling, the weather and their families."

"And?" Markus prompted, his hand still rubbing Corin's hair in a deceptively calming manner.

And? And they spoke of the tyrant who overcharged their rent and neglected their welfare. Who kept them from advantages such as television, radio and telephones. Corin had never seen any of the things that were reputed to be enjoyed by certain territories. He'd only heard of the strict limitations of the economy he lived in. There was too little money and too much need. The population was sparse and the land unforgiving. Crops often died to severely dry conditions that depleted trade between districts and other territories, but Corin couldn't say any of this. Hearing of the disparaging opinions of the people he ruled over would doubtlessly anger the leader, and the only one there to take the brunt of his fury was Corin.

Fingers slid into the band of his collar and tightened, pressing the metal to his windpipe. "They talk about the laws and the delegates of their districts," Corin blurted out. "And...you."

"What do they say?" Markus asked, resuming the strokes of his hand.

Corin sighed inwardly. "They say you demand too much. That the rent is unreasonable and you won't listen to the delegates they send to negotiate solutions."

"And what do you think of their opinions?"

Corin forgot his subservience and looked up. "Master?"

Markus stared down at him, his dark brown hair in front fallen to just above his eyes. "Tell me what you think."

"What does it matter? I'm just a slave," he said with a tint of acid coloring his tone. He tensed and waited for the blow for the slight. Several seconds passed then, as if to prove the point of Corin's subservience, Markus unbuckled his belt and opened his pants to push them down to his thighs. Corin was too tired to resist. The emotional upheaval of the day had drained him of the strength to do anything other than obey.

He leaned forward and took the half-erect cock into his mouth, using his hands and lips to milk the length to its full potential. Markus sat back and placed his arms on the sides of the chair. With cool eyes that gave away nothing, Markus watched his slave tend his needs, as if he were merely a bystander. Corin applied pressure to all the areas that had pulled reactions from the leader before, cupping and rolling the ball sac in one hand while using his other to grip the base. He lowered his mouth as far as it would go without force and pumped the erection until his jaws began to strain with the effort of accommodating so much girth.

It was taking so long that he started to worry he wouldn't accomplish his goal. Many times during his training and for a while afterwards, the men he'd serviced would get annoyed with his inability to please them on his knees. They would bend him over and finish the job themselves, taking him brutally to punish him for his inadequacy. As wide as the leader felt sliding down his throat, he didn't want that cock pounding into him from behind with the driving pace of frustration.

He saw the first indication of the leader's imminent climax in the bunching of his muscles. Without warning, Markus' hands flew to his head and shoved him down so fast he had to work to control his gag reflex. Jets of seed shot into his stomach and when at last he'd swallowed it all, he slumped forward as his head was released.

"Use the bathroom then get into bed," Markus rumbled from above.

Corin stood on wobbly legs and went to relieve himself, a groan slipping past his lips afterwards when the soft mattress dipped to accept his weight. The leader joined him after stripping from his attire and cuffed his wrists in front. The blade that had been used to cut his clothes from his body was set onto the nightstand within easy reach and more cream was applied to the wounds on his back. While he was settled between Markus' legs with his head on the man's chest, he wondered about the questions he'd been asked earlier. There had been a purpose to them that had nothing to do with small talk, though he had not the slightest clue as to what that might be.

Eventually, the warmth surrounding him pulled him under and he fell from consciousness into a deep sleep.

Chapter Six

The next week followed much of the same routine, and Corin gradually descended into a state of reluctant acceptance. As Heather was constantly reminding him, he would get nowhere if he kept up his stubborn resistance. He quickly learned that the front door only opened to the voice commands of Heather and Markus, and stolen glances out of the windows on his trips to and from the bathroom revealed no means of escape via that route. His only option was to feign submission and hope that he would eventually be allowed out of the penthouse.

Some days, hope was harder to come by than others. His body was no longer his own. From the sensations he felt to his every movement, his Master controlled it all—even his arousal. Like clockwork after breakfast and lunch every day, he was held tightly while his cock was taken in hand. The abasement he'd initially felt at being groped in front of others slowly changed to the embarrassment of his reactions. Not only did he respond instantly to Markus' firm grip that coaxed him to the brink of climax, but he was unable to stop the silent pleading of his body for release. For long seconds afterwards, his pelvis would rock of its own accord, his erection screaming at the torture of being suspended time and again.

His Master seemed to take great satisfaction in watching the proof of his involuntary pleasure. Sometimes, all it would take was the pinching of his nipples or an exploratory finger in his ass while they showered together to elicit a response from him. It was like his body was one of the stringed instruments he'd read about, plucked this way and that to garner the desired response, no matter his personal wishes. The strain of the release trapped in his balls for hours on end became a constant, dull ache he was powerless to relieve.

Only in his mind was he able to take respite and dwell on his hatred for the man he called Master, though even then Markus had an uncanny knack for sensing his rebellion. With the sharp sting of the switch, his focus would be drawn back to the present. It never left more than light welts, and never broke his skin, yet was always enough to gain his attention.

Much to his internal loathing, he also eagerly awaited the leader's return at the end of each day. Throughout his life, he'd thought he'd learned to take nothing for granted, but he'd been wrong. He grew to cherish the liberty of sight and speech, readily answering his Master's questions about the guests at the hotel and their complaints about the laws and regulations.

Since the establishment rested near the border of the neighboring territory to the east, there had been many travelers from that area visiting to conduct business without their leader's knowledge. While trade was generally restricted to only that which the leaders of each territory approved of, the economy of the mid-southern territory was worse than theirs. Markus displayed special interest in the opinions of these travelers toward their ruling leader, wanting to know specific details, many of which Corin couldn't provide. If his lack of knowledge bothered the man, however, he didn't show it.

Corin waited now as he swallowed the last morsel of his breakfast, both anticipating and dreading what would come next. When his Master stood, he rose to follow, hesitating when the man continued past the center of the room. He hurried behind until Markus came to a stop in front of the bureau beside the bed. His cuffs were taken off and he watched warily as the bottom drawer was opened and neatly piled stacks of clothes were shown in place of the blankets which had previously occupied the space.

"You will keep your clothes here," Markus said as he pulled out a white T-shirt, jeans, underwear and socks and put them on the bed. "You will only wear these when you're out. If I find you dressed at any time in here, you will be punished. Shoes are to be kept by the door and Heather will show you where to do the laundry."

Corin's heart skipped with excitement. He let out a gasp in the next moment when the man yanked him forward by the back of his neck and grasped his flaccid cock in an iron grip. It wasn't painful, nor did it need to be. The message came in loud and clear, and he bowed his head in acknowledgment. "Yes, Master." He wouldn't do anything to warrant another week of total domination, at least not until he was sure he could escape without getting caught.

Markus' fist began to move up and down his member in slow, languorous strokes. The pace wasn't designed to bring Corin to the verge of orgasm, but apparently his body didn't know otherwise. He clenched his fists and closed his eyes as blood raced to fill his throbbing cock.

"If you take care of this without my permission, I will know. Now get dressed. You'll be accompanying Heather."

"Yes, Master," Corin panted, anything to make the teasing stop. Not until Markus let him go and the sound of the front door closing signaled the man's departure did he reach for his balls to massage the ache in them. While it wasn't nearly enough to ease the discomfort, he wasn't willing to risk the alternative of masturbation.

The clothes were brand new — a novelty to him — and fit surprisingly well. He took a few seconds to acclimate himself to being clothed again before walking to the kitchen where Heather was washing dishes. She turned around at the clearing of his throat and whistled, a huge grin splitting her face.

"Wow, you look like a whole new boy! How do the threads feel? Do you like them?"

Corin offered a tentative smile. He felt a kindredship toward her, although in many aspects, they were worlds apart. During the long hours she'd kept him company while doing her chores, he'd learned a lot about her. Despite the fact that she'd never been a pleasure slave, she had fallen in love with one once. When the man's Mistress had discovered their secret affair, she'd sold him to a Master known for his cruelty and Heather to a meat packing plant. By that time, Heather had already been pregnant. There, she'd birthed her baby and attempted suicide shortly after he'd been taken forever from her arms. That's when Markus had come to discuss business with the owner and found her in the infirmary. She claimed she still didn't know what had possessed him to buy her and give her a new life, but she was grateful, just the same.

Try as he might, Corin couldn't reconcile the Master he knew with the one who had saved her, but he'd ceased that effort some time ago. Heather's ability to find joy in the face of such tragedy gave him hope for his own life.

"I'll take that as a yes. Do you remember all the duties I explained to you?"

Corin shook his head, not wanting to lie, lest she make him prove it. Half of the time he'd been so caught up in his own thoughts that nothing else had mattered.

Heather laughed then clucked her tongue. "Just as well. It makes a huge difference when you can actually see what I'm talking about."

A knock sounded at the door and Corin got his first real look at the boy who had taunted him with hushed jeers and vicious jabs whenever Heather wasn't watching. Or man, rather. He was older than Corin would've guessed for his immature attitude, maybe a few years Heather's senior, with mousy brown hair and a tall, lanky frame. If it weren't for the black scowl distorting his features as he looked upon Corin, he might've been handsome in a fey sort of way.

"Is he leaving?" Josh asked Heather, jerking a thumb toward Corin.

"No, and don't you start. We've got enough work ahead of us without you causing trouble."

The man yipped when Heather swatted him on the butt then started dusting the furniture with a rag. Corin ignored his spiteful glares, confident that should Josh try something now, he could do more than helplessly put up with it. Heather gave him the full run down of the kitchen, showing him where everything was and giving him a daily schedule that would allow him to stay on top of the cleaning. It was nothing he wasn't already used to and had no problem keeping track. The cooking, however, was a different story.

Heather placed both hands on her hips and frowned. "You mean to tell me you've never cooked a single meal in your life? How did your mother ever put up with you?"

"My mother would rather have killed me than fed me," he mumbled without thought. "She taught my sisters how to cook."

The woman's eyes softened in sympathy and Corin had to look away. He'd long ago come to terms with his mother's hatred toward him and couldn't stand pity when he felt none for himself.

"Well, I'll just have to stay a little longer to train you in that, as well, but we'll get to it later. Put your shoes on. I'll take you down to the laundry room then show you around the compound. You'd best not try anything. Master is trusting me to watch over you, and if anything happens, it's my ass. Josh, you'll have to come back around noon. We're leaving," she called out as she gathered Markus' clothes from the floor and stuffed them into a narrow wicker basket behind the recliner.

Corin found a pair of durable sneakers next to the door and put them on, marveling at the snug fit. The size couldn't have been taken from his old pair. Those had been second-hand and far too large to keep on without strangling them with the laces.

"Amalie," Heather said, handing the basket to Corin. The door slid open and Josh shoved past them on their way out. He somehow managed to stomp at a near run as he sped down the hallway and took an exit opposite the elevator Corin hadn't noticed before. Heather simply sighed and shook her head.

"Is that your last name...Amalie?"

"Yes," she said, brightening "Oh, that reminds me. Master set the alarm to enable me to program your voice in there as well, but it'll only work to get in, so make sure you get all your outside chores done before you head back unless I'm with you."

Corin thought about that for a moment. It made sense that his Master didn't want him able to leave at any time, but...

"What if someone were to try to use me to get into his quarters? Isn't that a security risk?"

"Not really," she answered, pushing the button for the elevator. "It's set to detect levels of stress in your tone. When I first started working for him, it took me ages to get that damn thing open because I was so nervous."

When they stepped out onto the ground floor, he noticed the door leading to the massive area Markus had carried him through his first night there. "What's out there?"

"My, aren't you full of questions." Heather chuckled at his blush. "I don't mind. You've probably been storing them up for the past week. Master isn't exactly very sociable." They headed in the opposite direction down the long white corridor that seemed to go on forever. "That's the Market, where people from all over the territory come to trade their wares safely, buying and selling everything from soap to slaves.

You know... All that," she said, flipping her hand with a roll of her wrist.

"This corridor is soundproofed, though, to keep the noise out. There's another compound on the opposite side where deals with other territories are conducted, but there aren't many of those nowadays."

"Why not?"

Heather's brows knitted. "Haven't you heard of the contention between us and the people of the mid-southern territory? Their leader is trying to take over our lands. Master wants an alliance but not on the terms they're offering. We haven't actually gone to war yet, but there have been skirmishes."

Corin followed her absently, lost in thought over her words. Was that why Markus had taken him as a pleasure slave when he'd never owned one before? To privately glean information about his enemy from a boy who'd worked at a hotel that catered to residents of both territories? It made sense. Not even the taverns resting near the border would serve people from the neighboring area because of the fights that broke out over differences of opinion. It explained the numerous questions he was asked night after night, and the reason why the leader never got upset while hearing about the enmity those people held for him. What better way to win over an enemy than to find out what they wanted and propose a better deal than what they had?

Markus had simply seen a golden opportunity in him and seized it. Corin wanted to believe that was the only reason he'd been taken. If that were the case, then eventually he would be discharged from service once his knowledge ran dry—or at the very least elevated to a work slave. He wanted to think that was the case and tried desperately to ignore the twist in his gut which told him otherwise. There was something about the way the man touched him, played his body and bent his will that gave him the impression he would not be released so easily.

They passed through the door at the end of the corridor and entered a large auditorium filled with rows of tables flanked by benches and chairs alike. The room was also predominantly white, though the floors were scuffed and the expanse of the walls broken by the occasional canvas depicting open landscapes and men in poses of stature. A long stainless steel cafeteria line stretched out across more than half of the wall to the left. In the center were a few clusters of men who sat at some of the tables playing card games. Thankfully, none paid any more attention to them than a bored glance.

"This is the commons room where most of the men who work for Master take their meals or hang out when they're off duty," Heather was saying as she veered to the right toward a door in the corner on the opposite wall. "You'll be joining Master here for supper tonight, but don't expect any food while you're kneeling at his feet. Slaves aren't allowed to eat with everyone else."

Of course not, he thought sarcastically. *It's bad enough we pollute the air just by breathing.*

By the time they left the large room, his muscles were beginning to feel fatigue, unused to exercise after so long in confinement. They entered a vast, empty kitchen then exited almost immediately through a side door on the right. He sighed in relief at the sight of several industrial washers and put the basket down.

Heather gave him a lopsided grin. "Not so fast, tough guy. Master likes his clothes washed separately. You'll understand once you see some of the men at dinner tonight." She shivered dramatically, leading him past a half dozen slaves engrossed in their work and around a corner to a smaller area with six washer and dryer units stacked atop one another. With practiced efficiency, she taught him how to use the machines and the special care needed for leather items.

After setting the timer, they left to visit the pantry at the back of the kitchen but didn't get that far. A group of four men stood in their path on the other side of the laundry room door. Heather bowed her head in docility, an act that seemed completely out of character with her normal countenance and took a single step in retreat. Corin couldn't understand the sudden, fine tremors that shook her slim frame until one of the men walked forward and placed his hands on either side of the door at her back, effectively trapping her.

The man was swarthy, with dark skin and hair that reeked of stale cigars and machinery oil. He leaned in close and Heather turned her head to the side with a grimace only Corin could see. "What have we here? It's nice to see you again, darlin'."

"Mo, you shouldn't be in here—"

"And she has a new friend," one of the other men cut her off. "It's about time. I was getting tired of that whiny little bitch who usually follows her around."

For a moment, Corin could do nothing except avert his gaze as the man advanced on him then bite the inside of his cheek as his nipples were twisted savagely. He was so used to being dealt this type of behavior that his response was automatic. At the hotel, he hadn't dared fend off the assaults for fear that the guests would take insult and submit complaints, which would earn him beatings. If his stepfather happened to witness the assaults, he would merely sell Corin's services to them and, if that was refused, accuse Corin of trying to earn his own money and beat him, regardless.

But he wasn't at the hotel and his Master had voiced no inclination to share him with others. Corin smacked the hands from his chest and bared his teeth.

"He's a feisty one, too," the man said in an amused tone. "Don't you know the rules, boy? You strike me and I can take restitution by owning you for the night."

Before he could move, the man shoved Corin so hard into the nearest wall that his head cracked on the painted brick. Fingers dug into his arms in a bruising grip and he cried out when a knee was jammed painfully into his groin.

"He's my Master's new boy and off limits," Heather spat out.

The man withdrew so quickly Corin nearly lost his balance.

"But you're not, are you, sweet thing?" Mo asked. He lowered one hand to Heather's breast and squeezed it tightly, eliciting a soft cry from her. "I petitioned your Master again and imagine my surprise when he told me you'd made no request to leave his service for mine." He increased his grip, causing Heather to clench her fists to keep from twisting away.

"Let her go," Corin demanded in a tone that hid his rising panic.

"I've been nice so far," Mo went on, ignoring Corin's interruption, "but if you keep trying my patience, you'll regret it. I *will* have you." He pulled his hand away and slapped her hard enough to leave a vivid handprint. "Don't make me wait." The other men followed him out of the kitchen, throwing out lewd comments on their way.

Heather was shaking uncontrollably now and when Corin reached out a hand, she flinched away from it. "Heather—"

"Don't," she snapped tightly. Tears glistened in her crystal blue eyes, but she held them in. After taking a few deep breaths, she reversed directions and reentered the laundry room.

Corin jogged to keep up with her as she marched to a back exit that opened to a white hallway lined with doors. She led them through a labyrinth of seemingly random turns, each door she took depositing them into another hallway similar to the last, until they finally entered one he was familiar with only because of its inordinate length.

Heather punched the buttons on the elevator and when they reached the top floor, barked out the command to open the door to Markus' penthouse. Once inside, Corin couldn't hold back any longer.

"Why did you let him touch you like that?"

"It's none of your concern," Heather ground out, before picking up a washcloth and scrubbing viciously at one of the countertops.

"But you're Master's slave, too. Why am I off limits and you aren't?"

"Because I'm not his fuck toy!" she shouted.

Corin recoiled as though struck then quickly swallowed down his offense. She was only lashing out to cover the shame cracking through her tough exterior. He'd wanted to do it enough times in his past that the signs were blaringly obvious to him.

"You're untouchable because he's taken a personal interest in you."

"But didn't he take one in you, as well? Don't you think he would defend you if he knew what was going on?" He was stretching his opinion of the man—by a landslide—but Heather thought the world of Markus and that had to stand for something, didn't it?

The woman's body seemed to deflate as a single tear trickled down her cheek. "I don't know, and I'm too afraid to find out. You heard that guy. If I strike back, Mo could claim punitive damages and demand my services for a day. And if the offense were great enough, he could request the right to buy me altogether. I just can't take the risk that Master won't stand up for me. Please don't tell him."

Anger burned in his chest at the futility of her plight. It wasn't fair, but then so little was when it came to the rights of slaves. A knock sounded and Heather called out her command to admit Josh. The man halted just inside the door and looked from her to Corin with a frown.

"What happened?"

"Nothing," Heather lied, wiping at the tear that had fallen. "I'll need you to go fetch the laundry we started."

Josh studied her face, most likely taking in the palm print that still marked it, and snorted. "It was Mo again, wasn't it? Why don't you just give in and let him buy you? At least then you'll have someone that wants you."

Corin's jaw dropped in shock. He'd known the guy was a jerk, but that was above and beyond his normal level of assholishness. "How can you say that?"

"What?" Josh asked, raising his hands in a gesture of confusion. "He'll find a way to get her eventually, and God knows she needs to get laid."

Corin's mind blanked out. He took two steps, swung his arm and smashed his fist into the other man's jaw. Before Josh could hit the floor, he grabbed onto his shirt and slammed him against the door. "You ever say anything like that again and I'll make you scream for mercy."

"Amalie," Heather called.

The moment the door slid open, he shoved Josh through and watched the man scramble away with a look of defiant retribution on his face. When the door closed again, he shook out his fist, teeth grinding in fury.

"You know you'll be punished if he tells Master."

Corin shrugged. He had no problem with defending others. It was himself he couldn't muster the confidence for. "It was worth it."

Heather paused then crossed the floor to kiss him on the cheek affectionately. "Thank you."

He smiled back. "You're welcome. So are we..."

"No." She shook her head. "The groceries can wait 'til tomorrow and Master's in a conference, so he won't be back for lunch. Go ahead and take your clothes off. I know about his stipulation regarding that."

Corin nodded as he moved to fold his clothes neatly on the bed then returned to help her with the rest of the chores. Josh came back sometime later with a bruise on his jaw and a surly attitude that neither of them paid attention to. At close to four-thirty, Heather took stock of the time and announced she had to leave.

"I need to help set up dinner for the men. Master will be here in about an hour to pick you up. Make sure you groom yourself first. He's a stickler for hygiene, as I'm sure you know. I'll see you tomorrow."

Corin waved as she left with a sulking Josh in tow. He took his time preparing himself for the meal, taking advantage of the privacy and freedom of movement. It felt like an eternity since he'd been able to just...be. The silence was peaceful instead of stifling, and the air clear of hampering emotions. He didn't even mind kneeling in front of the door when he was done to await his Master's return because it was his choice to make, not an order he'd received.

Small liberty, but a liberty, nonetheless.

When his Master came, Corin tried to tamp down his anxiety. The amount of tables in the commons area could easily seat two hundred people or more, and the only time he'd been around a crowd that large was during his brief trip through the market.

Markus patted him on the head, saying, "Get dressed, boy."

A measure of weariness leaked through the man's voice and Corin wondered if the conference he'd attended had anything to do with the war. He dressed in the same outfit and put on his shoes, holding still as his wrists were cuffed behind his back. Keeping a two-pace distance behind his Master, he followed as they made their way to the commons area. Several men and women came out of the doors in the corridor to join them on their path and he realized they were coming from their own rooms. Judging from his earlier excursion and the amount of hallways he'd passed through, this entire section of the building must be made up of living quarters.

The echoing volume that hit him when they entered the auditorium was near deafening. Soldiers of all ages milled about the tables, biding their time with various methods of entertainment. Most stood or sat and talked boisterously while others looked to be holding physical competitions he was unfamiliar with. Two men surrounded by a cluster only five yards from him pulled out their knives and began slashing at each other with such speed the glinting metal was a blur. Corin shrank back, wide-eyed, when the men came within inches of slicing through flesh then clapped each other on the back. The crowd around them roared their approval, while slaves carrying all manner of cookware and utensils steered well clear of the commotion.

Corin jerked at the large hand that snaked through his hair and wrapped around the back of his neck. Markus loomed over him, his dark brown eyes unfathomable, yet lacking the cold distance he usually associated with them. One corner of the man's mouth quirked up and Corin got the distinct impression he was amused.

"Am I going to have to attach a leash to you?"

Corin shook his head, realizing only then that his feet had rooted themselves to the floor. "No, Master."

Apparently satisfied with that response, Markus continued to weave through the throngs of people, and Corin was grudgingly grateful for the hand that remained at his neck and the solid build of the man at his side. They came to a round table against the far right wall, already full to capacity except for one chair, which Markus sat in, guiding Corin to kneel between his legs underneath the table. From his view, it was possible to see slaves at other tables kneeling in the same fashion at the feet of their Masters, although there were very few. He started to wonder why when he saw that most of them were going through the cafeteria line and serving the plates to the crowd.

The volume quieted as the food was served. Corin shifted to try to find a comfortable position on the hard, linoleum floor, but stilled when his Master's fingers curled around the curve of his collar. When small tidbits came to him from Markus' other hand, he ate them without hesitation. The food was delicious and his empty stomach gave him little choice. He was briefly surprised that his Master would break the rule about feeding slaves in the commons room, though he suspected Markus was doing so secretly.

After a while, he began to distinguish the voices of the men around the table he was at, noticing that his Master's own voice rarely joined theirs and never in a humorous manner. From the way people warmly greeted and spoke to him, Corin was sure the man's aloofness couldn't be for lack of friendships.

What must it be like to be surrounded by people who respect you and never find joy in their company?

The running feet of a man nearing them distracted him from his thoughts and he watched as they came to a skidding halt next to Markus' chair.

"Sir, there's been a breach in the other compound," the guard whispered with alarm in his tone.

Markus' chair flew back so fast it toppled over. At a command Corin couldn't see, the soldiers at his table and the one next to it jumped up and ran after Markus toward the corridor leading to the Market. A nervous hush settled over the crowd at the abrupt departure of their leader and the select group. Corin glanced around, unsure of what to do. The urge to sneak away and make a run for it came and passed just as quickly. The room was still teeming with people and he wouldn't get far, regardless, with his wrists bound. He thought about going back to Markus' penthouse, but

Heather had yet to program his voice into the alarm system.

So he remained — and waited.

Chapter Seven

Thirty minutes later, people began to vacate the commons area, and an hour after that, only servants were left to clean up the mess. He was beginning to think he'd been forgotten when angry shouts filled the relative silence. Corin peered out from beneath the table and froze. Flanked by a group of men in various states of disrepair was Markus. Blood was splattered across his clothes and face and the fury radiating from him in waves caused Corin to shrink back under the cover of the table. It sounded as though they were contending with each other. Accusations flew and tempers flared until he thought a fight might break out among them.

Markus' booming voice rose above them all, coming toward him with frightening speed. It was all he could do not to bolt when the chair in front of him was tossed aside and the table flipped onto its top. He was snatched up by his arm and scrambled to stay on his feet as Markus hauled him from the commons area.

When they entered the corridor, one of the men stopped and made a piteous plea, "Sir, you have to believe me. I had no idea."

Markus whipped around, yanking viciously on Corin's arm with his momentum. He grabbed the other man by the throat and bashed his head into the wall. "You *hired* him! If our security goes down, I will personally find you and rip you apart." Throwing the man to the ground, he stalked over to the elevator with the others on his heels. "You're off duty until we find out exactly what happened. Double the guards. I want men at every station, entry and exit."

The trip to the top floor was crowded and filled with shouts competing in volume, but when the doors opened again, Markus was the only one talking. He stepped out, turned on them and in a deadly voice said, "Find the missing man, no matter what it takes. I will *not* have a traitor among us."

Once inside the penthouse, Markus dragged Corin over to the foot of the bed and released him. Corin didn't bother to keep his eyes cast downward and, instead, watched warily, shaking so hard it was almost impossible to draw in breath while Markus paced the width of the room. The man clawed at his hair then spun and punched the wall, leaving a ragged crater where his fist had been. After several seconds, he turned his blazing glare on Corin, as if suddenly remembering he was there.

Corin stumbled back as his Master stalked toward him, searching with wild eyes for a way out and finding none. Markus unfastened the cuffs from his wrists then tore the shirt from his chest.

"Get undressed."

Corin tried to comply while the man stripped out of his own clothes, but his hands were trembling too much to work the button of his pants. *Please, no,* he wanted to beg, unable to push the words past the constriction of his throat. He was excruciatingly aware of his Master's size and knew he would be ripped apart if he was taken with the force of the man's rage.

Markus snarled impatiently and tossed him onto the mattress. Before he could think to struggle, Corin was completely naked and pulled into the bathroom. Markus turned on the shower jets and as soon as the temperature was adjusted, Corin was yanked inside and taken into a fierce embrace. A hand clutched onto his hair, wrenching his head back and the gasp that tried to come out was swallowed by Markus' mouth. Shock rendered him motionless as a demanding tongue pushed past his lips and dove in.

He had no idea what to do, never having been kissed before. It was almost painfully intimate, being so close to another person that he could breathe in the air from their lungs, taste the fuel of their desire. He'd seen others kiss and dreamt of a time when he would get his own chance, but his fantasies had never included this scenario. A ripple of anger coursed through him at the knowledge that this was one more first which had been stolen from him, one more theft he couldn't prevent. As Markus' tongue quested along the recesses of his mouth, he braced himself against the urge to fight it. He was a slave, and this was just another sacrifice in his bid to stay alive.

Markus broke away and lifted him, saying, "Wrap your legs around me."

Corin did so, curling his arms around the man's neck to hold on and feeling the stiff length of Markus' arousal at his crevice. His mouth was once again plundered and he tried to duel with the tongue dominating his to please his Master, but was too uncoordinated. Finally, he simply gave up and yielded to the deep swipes drinking him in. Markus hitched him higher and pressed a finger to his clenched hole. It pushed in with wet ease, delving farther than it had each morning during their showers together. Another finger was added and Corin winced at the stinging burn. They speared in and out of his entrance, stretching him and burying deeper into his canal with each pass.

They twisted around and hooked forward, hitting something that sent sparks of electricity shooting down his spine. Corin shivered, holding on tighter as that spot was rubbed again and again until he was panting into Markus' mouth. He wanted to ask what was going on, but didn't dare speak, not even sure he could if he'd been given permission. In all the years of being forced to submit to intrusion, nothing had ever elicited a reaction like this. It felt wonderful and terrifying at the same time. His cock swelled with an overpowering rush of blood and ached with the friction of skin gliding along every hard inch of it.

When the fingers were replaced with the thick head of Markus' erection, fear swept in and swiftly quelled the pleasure. Corin tensed, preparing himself for the pain of entry, but it never came. Instead, Markus growled and lowered him to his feet.

"On your knees, boy," he said hoarsely.

Corin dropped down, confused at the unexpected change of mind yet not about to argue. Taking Markus' protruding member in one hand, he circled the head with his tongue then brought his mouth forward. It was so engorged that he could trace the pulsing veins along its underside as the tip reached the back of his throat. Markus was too far gone for the languorous worship he usually preferred, so Corin set up a fast pace, humming around the thick cock stretching his mouth wide and swallowing as much of it as he could.

"Touch yourself," Markus ordered raggedly from above.

Corin paused and pulled back in surprise. "Master?"

The man's hooded eyes raked him with blatant lust. "Stroke yourself like you would your Master. Tight and fast."

Markus' hips bucked forward, his cock bobbing against Corin's lips and pushing forward as they opened. Hesitantly, Corin reached down to take hold of his own member, still straining from the previous stimulation. It took only a few strokes before the impact of his firm touch bowled through him. So many times he'd been handled mercilessly by his Master, brought to the edge of orgasm and denied until he couldn't think straight for the pressure that had built in his groin with no means of release. His body came alive as if it'd been trained to perform in a way only Markus could control.

"Don't you dare come without permission, boy." Markus grabbed onto his head with both hands and rammed his cock in to the hilt. His thrusts were grueling as he clenched his fists in Corin's hair and buried himself as deep as he could go.

Corin clasped onto one large thigh for balance while he stroked harder with his other hand. Fire lanced through his blood and he moaned wantonly, so immersed in the incredible sensation of milking his pleasure that nothing else mattered—not the hands gripping him almost painfully or the cock stretching his throat. His balls pulled in tight with his imminent release and he moaned louder, wordlessly begging his Master for permission before it was too late.

"Fuck," Markus grunted as he pounded faster. "Now!"

Corin's body exploded as soon as he heard the command. His climax tore through him with the force of a torrent as his cry was smothered by the throbbing cock filling him and spurting thick streams of cum into his mouth. It seemed to last forever, the tension of being forced to wait so long making his body tremble with aftershocks. Gratitude bubbled up and it took several moments for the fog to clear from his mind to realize how perverse that emotion was toward the man who owned him. He wanted to dredge up his constant enmity for his Master but couldn't find the strength.

Markus lifted him and allowed him to lean back against the wall once his legs decided to work. The leader's hands gently glided over his chest, neck and arms, and Corin rolled his head to look down at the spot where those hands stilled. There were four dark fingerprints banding his biceps from where it had been grabbed earlier. He flicked a glance up and saw Markus' brow creased in a frown before following his Master's gaze to his other biceps and the still noticeable marks left from the man in the kitchen.

"Who touched you?" Markus asked in a voice so low it was hard to hear over the running water.

Corin bit his lip and looked to the floor. He'd promised Heather not to divulge her predicament, but neither did he want to be punished for lying. "I-I don't—

"Who was it?" Markus asked, vehemently this time.

"I don't know!" And it was the truth. He hadn't caught the man's name and hadn't cared to.

"When?"

"This morning when Heather and I were taking the laundry to be washed." Corin held his breath, as wary of the man's unpredictability as he was his anger.

"You are *mine*, do you hear me?"

"Yes, Master," he said with a fervent nod, feeling his shoulders sag with relief. The tone had been one of pure possession, without malice or accusation. That, he could deal with.

Corin waited as his Master washed the remaining traces of blood from his body, not failing to notice that none of it was his. There was no talk afterwards as they climbed into bed and Corin's wrists were strapped into the cuffs. With his back mostly healed, Markus spooned him from behind and pulled him close, drifting off within a matter of seconds. Sleep eluded him, however, for several hours after that. He couldn't stop thinking about the man's lips pressed to his, the compulsion of his command and the subsequent, raging response it had drawn forth.

How could something so casual as masturbation become such an all-consuming act, and how could he do it again without recalling that kiss?

* * * *

Corin and Heather crouched side by side in front of the oven, at eye level with the surface of the chocolate cake sitting in a pan atop. They stared, unmoving, with critical eyes.

"I think it's...actually...deflating."

"I think so, too," Heather confirmed, slapping him on the back.

"Ow!"

"Don't worry. You've only been cooking for a few weeks and you already have the breakfast foods down. Give me the next month and you'll be an old pro."

Corin sighed inwardly and sat down at the table while Heather dumped his latest experiment into the trash. In one month, he would go insane with worry if he didn't find a way out. The stress of not knowing how his sisters were faring, of whether or not Scott was using them like he'd always threatened if Corin ever left, was becoming unbearable. Like a noose tethered to his emotions and strangling him from the inside.

Much to his surprise, Heather had recently been given permission by Markus to add his voice command to leave the penthouse as well as enter it. Yet, with the recent breach in security by spies from the neighboring territory, it was still impossible to make any attempt at escape. The guards were on high alert and Corin could go nowhere without eyes tracking his every move.

He looked over to Heather, the question he'd been hungering to ask hovering on the tip of his tongue. Over the short time he'd known her, she'd become a true companion, much like a third sister. She was so similar to Madeline, fearless in some aspects yet humble in others, that at times he couldn't stand it. She was the only one to treat him like a worthwhile human being in his new prison and he trusted her implicitly. If there was anyone who could help him escape, it was her.

"Heather..."

"Hmm?" She blew a stray lock of hair from her face while scrubbing the baking pan.

Gathering his courage, he blurted out, "How can I get out of here? You've got to know a way. You've been here for years. I'm not asking you to do anything, just point me in the right direction."

Her spine stiffened as she slowly turned to him, blue eyes shaded with reservation. "Why do you want to leave? Master is a good man."

Corin huffed in exasperation. "Because I was bartered for the debts of a man who should've paid for his own mistakes. Because I have sisters that I promised to protect. Because I am *not* another man's property! Take your pick."

Heather's grim expression softened with compassion. "You were property long before Master took you, were you not?"

Corin flushed at the harsh truth. She knew the only reason he hadn't been killed or sold at birth was because his mother and Scott had kept him as property. A slave to pander to their every whim, then later chained by the bonds of the love he held for his sisters when he might have left. Heather was right. He'd never been free, but he had felt a measure of freedom in his heart with his sisters, and he needed that back more than he needed air to breathe.

"Please," he whispered, not above begging. "I have to make sure my sisters are okay." Heather sighed and for a moment, he thought she might cave to his plight. For just a moment—then it passed. She lifted her shirt to her neck and turned around, exposing her back to him. It was a mass of scarred flesh made by some type of barbarous whip from the appearance. Many of the marks were puffy and knotted owing to the skin stretching and healing improperly.

Dropping her shirt back down, she turned again and fixed him with a resigned stare. "I tried to escape once when I was young. A man found me and used me in ways that should have made it impossible for me to ever carry a child before my Mistress found me and took me back. She punished me for days until I wanted to die, just to end the pain." She sat down in the chair next to his and touched his hand lightly. "I don't think Master would be so cruel if you ran away, but there are others out there who are. I just couldn't stand the thought of you being mutilated or murdered if I were to help you. I'm sorry."

Corin stared into her imploring eyes then sighed in defeat. He couldn't fault her for her reluctance. She truly did care about him and only wanted what she thought was best. He would have to find another way. "It's all right. I understand." When she didn't move, he plastered on a poor imitation of a smile in an effort to allay her concern.

Heather shook her head and stood. "Besides, you said your mother loves them, right? I'm sure they're safe with her. And they know who your Master is. When they're old enough, they'll find you. Just have a little patience."

Corin nodded weakly, his mind elsewhere.

"Come on. We need to go get some supplies before Master comes to pick you up for supper."

Dragging himself from the chair, he left to get dressed then met her at the door. Josh, *thank God*, had completed his working slave tutelage under Heather and been sent off on his own to attend to the domestic needs of some of the soldiers. It had been an immeasurable relief and one Corin felt every day.

They traveled down to the main corridor and through to the commons area. He wasn't nearly as intimidated as before when they passed by off-duty soldiers, wiling away their time with conversation and games. Most of them knew he was the leader's pet, having seen him with his Master every evening at dinner, and left him alone. There were still a few he tried to steer clear of for the malicious intent gleaming in their eyes—the ones he was sure would vie for Markus' position as leader if they had half the chance of succeeding. A small tendril of apprehension curled in his stomach at the prospect of Markus being replaced, though whether it was out of a desire to stay with Markus or fear of being forced to serve a stranger, he wasn't sure. Corin shook off those disturbing feelings and continued to follow Heather.

When they entered the kitchen, Heather handed him the cloth bag she'd grabbed before leaving and waved in the direction of the pantry. "Why don't you go get the supplies while I check on the laundry? It'll save us some time. You remember everything we need?"

Corin nodded and made his way to the other side of the kitchen while she took the side door to the laundry room. The pantry was located toward the back, next to the walk-in refrigerator. It was comparable to an average-sized grocery store and contained so many items there was a map on a pin board near the door with a listing of the various food types and where they could be found. He gathered the supplies they needed in short order then headed out to find Heather, pausing when he heard a chorus of loud voices.

Crude jeers reverberated along the walls of the expansive kitchen and he followed them to the entrance. A group of men he was regrettably familiar with circled like vultures around the object of their lustful taunts. Heather was tossed amongst them like a ragdoll, her hair now loose from its braid and used to tug her callously this way and that. Mo was the loudest of the men, slapping her breasts and ass hard enough to send her reeling into the others. Cowering in the corner next to the dishwashing basins was a petite young woman who looked to be about his age and of Asian descent. Her flowing black hair hid her face from his view and from the way she was wringing her hands, her fear was obvious. Whichever man she belonged to probably treated her with as much care as Heather was being treated now.

Corin gritted his teeth and approached, unwilling to stand quietly by in the face of such needless abuse. "Leave her alone," he yelled over the raucous laughter. The men quieted instantly and turned to sneer at him.

The man who'd assaulted him previously chortled darkly. "Stay out of this, bitch, before I tell your Master you've been a bad little boy."

"I don't care what you tell him," Corin said. "You *will* let her go." He took strength from the surprisingly level tone of his voice, though inside he vibrated with apprehension. Every one of Markus' soldiers contained an excessive amount of pride and an affront to it would result in a display of brawn at the very least. Add on stupidity to that and you had a deadly combination. The leader's pet he may be, but that status was hardly an invincible shield.

"Or what?" Mo asked, striding forward and shoving Corin in the chest. "You try anything and I'll break you so fast you won't have time to cry, just like I did my toy over there." He jerked his head in the direction of the cowering slave then shoved Corin again. "Not even Markus is immune to the rules, and he won't be able to protect you if you ever raise a hand to me." Spinning on his heel, he took three large steps and backhanded Heather so hard she fell to the floor in a desolate heap. "Just like he won't protect you. Right, darlin'?"

Corin's mind clouded with rage. He was so tired of this. Sick of the helplessness and the futility of a slave's life. Sick of the rules that beat them down as effectively as a Master's tool or fist. He saw the shame darkening Heather's eyes as she looked up at him, the oppressed posture of the slave in the corner, and decided the risk was well worth a day, or even a week, under Mo's ruthless attentions.

He snatched a half-full pot of coffee from the steel countertop next to him, ran forward and smashed it across the side of Mo's face. The man let out a curdling scream, the still-scalding liquid burning his flesh as small shards of broken glass sliced shallow cuts into his left cheek and nose.

There was a second of stunned silence then he said, "You bitch!"

Corin took off at a dead run, barreling past the men, through the kitchen entrance and weaving around the tables in the commons area. He could hear the pounding of boots racing after him, gaining speed as he pushed his body harder. Terror rushed through his entire being, but he forced himself to focus on one goal—Markus' penthouse. If he could just make it there before the men caught up to him, he could lock himself in. Just a little farther to the stairs opposite the elevator.

As he charged through the door leading to the corridor, he felt a hand claw at his shirt and looked back despite himself. Mo was almost on him. Grasping. Reaching.

Then his flight came to a crashing halt. Corin thought he'd run into a wall until a strong arm banded around him to keep him from toppling backwards. The scent of Markus' aftershave washed over him as he was picked up and swung around, catching Mo's frantic pursuit from the corner of his eye brought to an abrupt halt by a vicious jab to the throat by Markus.

"Stop!" Markus boomed.

Corin clung to the arm holding him, sure that his knees would buckle from the adrenaline pumping through his system like wildfire. The group of men that had chased him froze in their tracks, one of them helping up a coughing Mo from the floor. There were two men standing behind Markus with their arms crossed over their chests and feet spread, ready to defend their leader against even his own men.

"What's going on here?" Markus growled.

When Mo finally found his voice, tears streaming from the eye that had taken damage, he pointed a shaking finger at Corin. "That little bit—your boy," he quickly amended, "attacked me. Look at what he did to my face!" The man gestured sharply to the angry, red splotches on his skin.

Markus studied him briefly then brought Corin out from behind his massive frame. "Is this true?"

Hell yeah, it's true! he exclaimed inwardly and swallowed past the dryness in his throat to force the words out. "Yes, and I'd do it again if I had the chance." They came out barely above a whisper and lacked the conviction he felt, but they sufficed. When his Master arched a brow at him, he summoned his courage and turned a defiant glare on Mo. "He was hurting Heather, trying to provoke her into hitting him so he could stake a claim on her." Guilt speared him at the confession of a secret he'd sworn to keep, even as he realized it was a moot point by now.

The leader looked back, beyond the group to the two women Corin hadn't noticed were standing just inside the doorway to the corridor. "Heather, come here."

She walked hesitantly toward them, insecurity slowing her every step. The men shifted to let her pass, though Mo shot her a look of such vengeance that Corin thought she might turn and run. When she was close enough, Markus took her chin in hand and tilted her head up, surveying the cut on her bottom lip, tear tracks and handprints coloring her cheeks.

"Did Mo do this to you?"

Heather let out an inarticulate sound then whispered, "Yes, Master."

The leader nodded grimly. "Take Corin to my quarters then go to your own. Stay there until I call on you."

"Yes, Master."

Corin took her proffered hand when Markus let him go and walked down to the elevator, the vile accusations and demands for reparation from Mo ringing in their ears until the doors sealed them in.

"I'm sorry," Corin said in a rush. "I didn't mean for things to get so out of hand." His guilt rose when Heather didn't respond. Her shoulders were slumped inward and her head was bent as if her very spirit had deflated. In silence, she walked him to the penthouse and left as soon as he was inside.

He stared at the door for a time, trying to quell the crushing anxiety in his chest, and eventually made his way to the bed where he undressed and placed his folded clothes on the side. After putting his shoes in their spot near the entrance, he knelt on the hardwood floor and waited with his hands behind his back, eyes to the polished planks beneath him.

Chapter Eight

Corin's mind, for once, took mercy on him, obscuring his racing thoughts and allowing his retreat into a state of blankness. Time passed without measure, the ticking of the grandfather clock a lulling background noise rather than a countdown to the judge's verdict. When Markus finally came, the anticipatory stuttering of his heart was merely daunting instead of incapacitating.

His Master pulled him up by the collar and led him to stand at the foot of the bed. He bound the cuffs to his wrists in front then took a step back. Through his lowered lashes, Corin watched Markus take the gun harness from around his wide shoulders and the sheath from his belt and place them on the lamp table.

"Do you know why you're being punished?"

"Yes, Master."

"Then tell me."

Corin furrowed his brow at the odd command. "Because I struck a free man."

"No, because you lied to me," Markus rumbled in his resonant voice.

Corin's frown deepened and he flicked a glance up at his Master's rugged, implacable features. "I don't understand."

Markus walked over to the nightstand to retrieve something from the drawer then removed his boots and socks and set them to the side. "You were upholding the law, my law, that a working slave will not be held accountable for their actions while defending themselves, provocation aside. You defended Heather when she couldn't, which is the only thing that saved you from a night with Mo. However, she informed me that this wasn't the first time she's been victim to Mo's pursuance, and that you were there to witness his assault on at least one other occasion. Yet instead of informing me of this, you took matters into your own hands."

Corin flushed with relief, then felt panic spiral in its wake as he saw the thick, leather belt being pulled from the loops of his Master's pants and wrapped around one large hand.

"Lies breed dissention, and I won't tolerate that among my men, let alone from my boy."

Then why do you keep me? he wanted to shout. They both knew he'd run dry of useful information about the guests at the hotel, and his disobedience was a risk Markus couldn't afford. The leader needed to put up an infallible front in order to keep the respect of his men, especially now that there was a war brewing on his doorstep. Corin was nothing more than a needless distraction when Markus could simply rent slaves for his pleasure.

Markus stepped close and for a moment, tenderness softened his features. "What you did was very brave — and foolish. I won't let you put yourself in harm's way, no matter the circumstance."

While possession filled Markus' voice, there was also something else. Something deeper that made Corin suspect his coming punishment was not just a lesson in obedience. His Master wore an expression he hadn't seen before on the man. Was that fear glinting from the depths of his eyes? No, it couldn't be. Why would a man with such power be afraid for the well-being of a slave? Still, Corin couldn't shake the impression that Markus was more disturbed than he was letting on.

Corin straightened his shoulders and replied with an edge of defiance, "I'd do it again if I had to."

To Corin's surprise, a corner of Markus' mouth lifted in a slight grin. "I'll deal with Heather's punishment later. For now—"

"No!" Corin snapped his head up, forgetful of his submission until he saw the reproach in his Master's eyes. "I'm sorry. I mean… She doesn't deserve to be punished. She was just afraid to tell you. I was the one who should've said something."

"Are you saying you're willing to take her punishment for her?"

Resignation curled in his gut. With his eyes glued to the belt hanging from the man's hand, he answered, "Y-yes, Master."

Markus caught his jaw and lifted it, though Corin kept his gaze on the man's stubbled chin. "Brave, but it's not for you to decide."

"Please."

"Enough," Markus said in a tone that brooked no argument. He looped the belt through the chain linking the cuffs together then pulled it down to the metal leg holding up the nearest corner of the bed. He tied the loose end around the leg, giving Corin only about a foot of lead. Corin knelt, biting his tongue, while his Master sat on the foot of the mattress then hefted Corin's backside up so that he was lying across the man's lap. His ass pointed awkwardly toward the ceiling and one of Markus' legs moved to straddle both of his behind the knees while the front of his limp cock pressed into Markus' thigh.

With his arms pulled taut and his legs trapped, it was all he could do to tamp down his growing alarm and pull air into his lungs. His Master's hands caressed his back, ass and thighs in an almost soothing manner that only served to heighten his awareness.

"I will not harm her," Markus said calmly. "She's served me faithfully for many years and has suffered enough from Mo."

A sliver of gratitude wormed its way past the barrier of his anxiety. Not for the man's decision to spare Heather, he had a feeling Markus had already made up his mind as to how he would punish her, but for the unnecessary admission to ease his worry. It made a difference, and he suspected Markus knew that.

The man's hand came down on his ass without warning—sharp and solid, with an impact that rocked him against the leg that supported him. Searing heat spread along his buttocks as a second strike landed, then a third. Corin bit his lip against the flashing pain. He'd been spanked before, numerous times, but it'd felt nothing like this. It was as if his skin was being pounded by a steel paddle, hitting him with such force that it knocked the breath from his clenched throat. He counted to keep his mind focused, but after the tenth blow, his thoughts scattered.

Corin screamed and fought to break free, struggling in vain desperation. One hand pushed between his shoulder blades to hold him still while the other rained down a methodical flurry of strikes upon his ass and the backs of his thighs. He cried out for mercy and begged forgiveness until his voice was too hoarse to do anything more than sob. Hot tears ran unchecked through his lashes and into his hair.

He didn't know when it finally ended, his awareness slow to return as Markus' hands smoothed over his sensitized flesh, kneading his buttocks on occasion and causing more anguished sobs to escape. The tortured mounds of his ass were pried apart and a slick finger grazed over the bundled nerves at his entrance before pushing in. The sting of the invasion was nearly unremarkable in comparison and he made no effort to move away, utterly drained of energy.

It slid in and out with an ease that could only come from lube and, seconds later, another was inserted. They stretched his tight ring, circling around and loosening his entrance to make way for a third. The burn increased as their width spread him open, twisting against the resistance of his grasping muscles. Then they hooked forward and hit that spot that caused sparks to shoot up his spine. They rubbed it repeatedly, luring uncontrollable arousal from the depths of his pain. His hushed sobs turned to whimpers as his body flooded with new sensations.

It had been a while since his Master had let him come. Every day, many times a day, he would bait Corin's orgasms with the brush of his fingers over that spot or the pumping of his cock to a straining erection. More often than not, he would deny Corin release, making him suffer until the desire to come was nearly an insatiable need. The past several days of denial had built a mountain of pressure that rushed to the surface, demanding to be released despite the throbbing ache in his backside.

Or perhaps because of it.

The deep-seated heat in his bruised backside seemed to meld with the streaks of pleasure, creating a combined force that set his blood to racing. When the fingers pulled out, he almost groaned at the emptiness they left behind. Markus leaned over and his hands dropped to the floor when the belt was undone. He was picked up and draped, belly side down, onto the soft comforter. The bed shifted under Markus' considerable weight and Corin's midsection was lifted, a pillow pushed under his pelvis. He knew the inevitable was coming. For three weeks the leader had restrained himself, heeding the cautionary words of the doctor who'd inspected Corin the night of his arrival, but that was at an end now. Corin was healed and more than capable of fulfilling his Master's needs, in body if not in mind.

There was a shuffling of clothes behind him then the massaging squeeze of fingers on his bruised ass. He groaned, trying to inch away unsuccessfully. The leader's knees pushed his thighs far apart, exposing his quivering hole and causing his body to shiver as cool air wafted down his cleft. Warmth immediately replaced it as Markus lay down over his back and pressed the tip of his leaking head to Corin's entrance.

Corin tensed, breath quickening as he was slowly breached. Inch by inch, his Master's heavy erection drove into him, expanding his insides until he thought no more could fit. It continued to snake deep into his gut, stopping only when coarse hairs scratched his abraded flesh and balls tapped lightly against his. Scrunching his fists into the blanket, he panted and fought to remain still and relax his muscles. He would only bring damage to himself if he didn't loosen his bracing muscles.

"Shh. Easy," Markus crooned close to his ear, gliding his hands over Corin's trembling body. He began to swivel his hips then withdrew his rigid length until only the tip remained inside.

Corin gasped as the head grazed over the spot within his passage. His Master plunged back in with a grunt then pulled away again, brushing that nub and sending ripples of pleasure that matched the sharp pain. Markus gradually increased the force of his strokes, sinking himself so far into the depths of the channel that clutched him that Corin couldn't think past the pressure rapidly building within.

"Damn, you feel so good." Markus lunged harder. "I always knew you would." And faster. "Since the first time I saw you."

Corin heard the words and tried to make sense of them through the haze that enveloped his mind. The mixture of the pain on the outside and the consuming pleasure increasing within was like an irrepressible tide pushing him past his limits. He tightened his hold on the blanket and pressed back, meeting his Master's pummeling thrusts with an uncontrollable eagerness. The friction of the pillow on his swollen member revved his yearning need until all that mattered was attaining his release.

Markus pulled him up by the chest so his back came to the man's front and brought him crashing down. Corin cried out and tried to get away, the new angle forcing his ravaged ass down painfully onto Markus' hips, but the man only strengthened his hold. He banded one arm across Corin's shoulders, trapping his wrists to his chest, then fisted Corin's erection in an iron grip with his free hand. Markus plunged into him with aggressive strokes while pumping Corin's pulsing shaft in strong, furious pulls.

"Come," Markus growled.

As though pulled from his body, his orgasm tore through him like a whirlwind. Corin shouted as his cock erupted, his climax bursting through him with driving speed. Distantly, he heard Markus yell as warmth bathed his insides. His head fell back and his body convulsed with tremors. The hand on his dwindling length milked every last drop until he whimpered with sensitivity. Gently, he was laid back down and his Master's cock slipped from his ass.

Too tired to keep his eyes open and too sore to move, he lay there listening to sounds he couldn't make sense of coming from the direction of the Jacuzzi. Seconds, or possibly hours later, he was lifted then immersed in a pool of hot water. With a weak cry, he scrambled to get out, but was held firmly against his Master's broad chest.

"Easy, boy. Settle down."

The words vibrated along his skin, offering respite as much as the heat soaking into his aching muscles. They tugged at the back of his mind, evoking a spark of confusion, but it was gone before he could latch onto it. The last thing he felt as he gave up the struggle for consciousness was the press of firm lips to his forehead, nose and mouth.

* * * *

Corin blinked open his eyes, squinting against the bright morning rays cascading in through the nearby window. He pulled the covers over his head, rolled over and gasped at the flare of pain in his backside. It took only a moment for his disorientation to pass and the events of the day before to spark fresh in his memory. Heather, Mo, the coffee pot and his subsequent punishment. Not the sentence he might have received, according to Markus, for which he still felt a measure of relief. As much as he hated and feared his Master, the man was familiar, even in his unpredictability. Mo, on the other hand, was... Corin shivered in revulsion. He'd been right. His sacrifice had been well worth the crime.

Only that's not what he'd been punished for. It had been for lying to his Master.

Corin scraped the hair from his face and looked around frantically, realizing only then that there were no arms holding him in place—no cuffs at his wrists. After crawling out of bed, he hobbled over to the bathroom and, finding it empty, made his way to the kitchen. Heather was peering under the sink and humming softly to herself in the way he'd become familiar with. He cleared his throat and frowned as the woman turned and jumped up with a huge grin. She rushed over and tugged him into an exuberant embrace, then pulled back to assess him critically.

"How are you feeling?"

His voice cracked and he cleared his throat again, wincing at the ragged soreness. "I'm fine. Where's Master?"

"He left an hour ago. Told me to let you sleep in."

"He did?" When Heather nodded, Corin searched her face for any signs of distress. "Are you...? Did he hurt you?"

She smiled sadly. "No. He only assigned me some extra chores to do throughout the week, but I know you didn't get off as easily. Turn around so I can see the damage."

"I'm fine, really." That argument held up for the span of exactly one heartbeat. Heather crossed her arms over her chest and gave him a look only

Madeline had been able to pull off on him. He sighed and turned around, standing still as she bent to inspect his bruised ass and thighs. Even the light touch of her finger pads felt like nails scratching along his skin.

"Well, there's not nearly as much swelling as I would've expected," she said. When he turned back to face her, guilt furrowed her brow. "I'm sorry I asked you to keep Mo's behavior a secret from Master. I should've told him from the start. It's my fault you were dragged into this."

Corin shrugged with a smile. "It's all right. I don't blame you." And he didn't. He more than most knew how hard it was to trust in the moral judgment of a Master when slaves were given no rights to justice. No matter how much that Master might seem to care.

With a smile of gratitude, Heather turned to pick up a small jar from the counter next to the refrigerator. "Did he let you soak in hot water?"

Corin remembered the punishment, the shock of hot water and what had come in between. The sting of penetration, the ache of the pummeling thrusts and his response to it all. Heat flushed his cheeks and he looked away. For the first time, he'd not simply taken what had been forced upon him, he'd actively participated. Enjoyed it. The cravings of his body had been so powerful that not even the pain had hampered his need.

"Not all punishment then, hmm?"

He glanced up to find Heather smirking, her eyes dancing with the truth that must have been written on his face. Corin spun on his heel and walked stiffly away, not stopping until his back was to the closed bathroom door.

"Corin? Hey, I'm sorry." Heather banged on the door. "Was it really that bad? I didn't... I mean, I thought maybe... I'm sorry."

He squeezed his eyes shut as he fought to contain his anger. She didn't know. How could she when she'd been a working slave her whole life? It was one thing to endure the inevitable, to lie down and submit to the brutal attentions of someone more powerful, but his pleasure had always been his to control. Last night, his Master had proven that he owned that, too. That he could take it at any time without Corin's permission, like he'd stolen every other freedom Corin had once taken for granted.

He thumped his head against the door and pushed back the swell of his emotions. He knew Markus had been conditioning his body since the first day, training him to react to his Master's touch, his command. And in truth, he had no right to feel possessive about any part of his body, including his reactions. He was a slave, and what was his belonged to his Master.

"Corin?" Heather banged again. "I have some cream to put on your bruises. Master said he applied it this morning but didn't want to wake you. He also wanted me to make sure you put more on throughout the day."

Taking a deep breath, he opened the door to find worry creasing the face of his friend.

"Did he really hurt you?" she asked. "I mean, aside from the punishment."

No, he hadn't. It had felt good. Amazing. And therein lay the problem. Corin shook his head and took the jar from her. "Thanks."

"I can put that on for you," she offered.

He gave her a droll stare then shut the door again. It was bad enough that she saw him in the nude every day. He didn't want her nursing him as well.

"Well, can I at least tell you what happened?" she called out.

"Am I going to be able to stop you?"

"Not a chance." She giggled.

Corin paused with a frown, not sure if he'd ever heard that particular sound come from her.

"Master was furious after we left. I could hear him shouting through the vents when I was walking back to my quarters. Okay, so I may have eavesdropped a little, but you wouldn't believe what he said. If Mo had laid a single hand on you for defending me, Master would have discharged him from service and banned him from the city. You should've heard the sniveling little idiot after that. Saying I wanted to be his slave and that you'd gotten the wrong impression."

Corin snorted. When nothing else came, he opened the door warily. "Did Master believe him?"

Heather was grinning madly and bouncing on the balls of her feet. "No. He was so angry, he stripped Mo of his rank and sent him and his friends to the other compound as guards to make sure they couldn't take retribution. And I have you to thank for it!" She hugged him tightly and kissed his cheek. "You have no idea how much this means to me. Thank you."

He nodded weakly, too stunned to do more. That his Master trusted Heather above one of his own men was conceivable, but that he would exile that man from the city for harming his boy was... Corin didn't know what to think about that. It seemed a bit extreme for possessiveness, but what else could it be? He was just a pleasure slave. Even when he'd been free, only his sisters had cared about his welfare.

On the other hand, maybe he was making too much of Markus' response. It only made sense that a man of the leader's stature would crush any further misconduct on the part of his men by taking such extreme measures. He had his reputation to uphold. Yet, more often than not, Corin had witnessed Masters completely dismiss the mistreatment of their slaves as if they couldn't be bothered to care. Not once had he seen a slave owner go to the lengths Markus had taken to protect their property.

His mind dredged up the memory of his first medical examination at Markus' behest and the restraint the man had shown in the shower just two weeks ago, when his channel hadn't yet healed completely. Corin shook his head. Markus had simply been ensuring the health of his investment. That was all.

Wasn't it?

"Hurry and finish up," Heather said as she went back to the kitchen. "I'll help you for a few hours, but after that, I need to leave so you'll have to do everything else on your own. With the amount of chores Master gave me, I'll be lucky if I can get more than an hour of sleep today. Oh, and he'll be stuck in meetings for most of the day, so don't forget to cook his supper when he gets back."

Corin finished applying the cream, surprised he was being allowed out of the penthouse after his earlier behavior. Heather remained in an exceptionally good mood throughout the morning, making sure to give him a simple recipe for the dinner he was to cook. Soon after she left, he pulled out clothes to dress in. Even the loosest-fitting pants, however, felt like sandpaper scraping over abraded skin as he tugged them on. It took him a while to travel down to the commons area with the laundry basket in hand. Every step added pressure to the sore muscles in his backside.

When he entered the kitchen, he couldn't help surveying the area of the altercation. It was immaculate, as if the scene had never occurred. Corin had always been slightly disturbed by that—how so much ugliness could be cleaned and easily forgotten. In the rooms at the hotel, no matter how much violence he had been a part of in them, the only evidence left behind was that which resided in his mind or on his body.

Not wanting to dwell on the issue, he went into the laundry room to start his load then took the grocery bag with him to the pantry. When he was finished, he started back for the penthouse to drop it off while he waited on the clothes. As he passed through the corridor, he heard an odd hissing sound come from an open door ahead and to his left. He slowed his steps and peered in, letting out a soft yelp when he was snatched inside by a delicate hand. The door shut swiftly and the little Asian woman he'd seen the day before in the kitchen stood before him.

She appeared even more fragile up close, with large, slanted black eyes and rosebud lips. Her porcelain skin and slim frame—a few inches shorter than his—made her an absolute beauty but for the dark, swollen bruises around her chin and one eye—courtesy of Mo, no doubt. Anxiousness sang from her trembling body and her gaze met his with earnestness.

"You want to go, no?"

Corin drew his brows down and put the bag on the floor. "What do you mean?"

"Leave. Go." She gestured toward the door. "You unhappy?"

He stilled as understanding began to seep in. "You mean escape?" When she nodded emphatically, he bit his lip, wondering if it was wise to trust her. Unlike his first assumption, there was no common bond among slaves. It was every man for himself, but the temptation to find out what she had in mind was too great to resist. "Yes."

She nodded again and pulled him into the small bathroom to the side of the door, looking around as if they might be caught at any second. "Four," she said, holding up four fingers, "go to market. Guards will be changing and not see you. Walk tall." The woman pumped up her shoulders and put her arms straight at her sides.

Corin nodded, nearly smiling at the way she embellished her broken English.

"Go to pole...umm, long..." She circled her fingers as though holding a ball and brought them up and down.

"Pillar?"

"Yes! Pillar with red flag by front door. There is brown truck. Get in back, under a blanket. Stay." She pointed a finger at him then waved both hands. "Don't move. Stay. Truck go to Wyntessen and stop there."

Wyntessen. That district was about an hour's drive north of the hotel, if he remembered correctly. It would be a long walk, yet not impossible. "Why are you doing this for me?"

The woman smiled then, and it lit up her whole face like moonbeams on a lily. She gave a mock punch to his temple, clasped his biceps in a remarkably strong grip and squeezed. "You good man. Stand up for lady. Not like my Master. Bastard."

Corin grinned when she turned her head to spit.

"Tell me…what it feel like?"

He thought for a moment, allowing his grin to become a full-on smile. "Good."

"Ahh!" The woman clapped her hands excitedly and laughed. "Thank you."

"What's your name?"

With a palm to her chest, she answered, "Mika."

Corin repeated the gesture, saying his name. He sobered then and slowly raised a hand to her swollen eye. "Come with me."

Mika shook her head. "Must get Master's things. He move."

"No, I mean, come with me to Wyntessen."

Her eyes widened impossibly and she took a step back, shaking her head adamantly. "No. I stay here. Out there…" She shivered once. "No."

Corin nodded and let it go. Her reaction to the proposal was too much like Heather's, which told him she likely had the same reasons for staying. With his hands held up in placation, he said, "Okay. Thank you for this, Mika. Thank you so much." He poured as much gratitude as he could into his words, knowing it still wasn't enough.

Mika smiled again and stepped forward, patting him on the cheek. "Be safe."

He nodded again and turned to leave but stopped when she made another odd hiss. Waving at his neck, she reached up and touched his collar. "Hide!"

Shit. He would've completely forgotten about that. Heather's words came back to him, reminding him that a slave without its Master could be picked up by

anyone. Nodding again, he scooped up the bag,
checked the corridor then left.

Chapter Nine

It was still early so he retraced his steps to the laundry room and completed the load before returning to the penthouse. Though the risk that Heather or Markus might show before he could make his escape was high, it was one he would have to take. Another chance might not come along for weeks or even months, and the thought of waiting that long only helped to steel his nerves.

Anticipation boiled in his blood like water in a hot spring. His body shook with a kaleidoscope of emotions, not the least of which was fear. He was trusting someone he barely knew, about to risk an escape during broad daylight and intentionally going against the authority of not only his Master, but the leader of the entire territory. He was lucky to have lived past his threat to the man's life his first night with him and was sure there would be no such forgiveness if he got caught. Markus' very reputation as a leader would demand no less than some form of debilitating punishment, if not death. In fact, Corin was positive he would prefer death if he failed.

But the hope that he would be able to see his sisters again predominated all else.

Focusing on the task at hand, he put away the food and laundry then cooked the prearranged meal for his Master. While not his best work, it was nevertheless passable. He wrapped and stuffed it into the fridge and wrote a note saying he was still working on the laundry and that he would be late. Whether his Master would buy it or not, he had no idea, but it might give him some time. He was going to need as much as he could get if he had to walk sixty miles to the hotel.

After cleaning only what was noticeably dirty, he found a small tote bag in the linen closet and filled it with it a change of clothes and some dry foods. With a rubber band, he tied back his white-blond hair, knowing it would be a dead giveaway, and donned one of Markus' sweatshirts with a hoodie he used to cover his head. It utterly dwarfed him but would have to suffice. From the nightstand, he took a watch Markus kept there and cinched it to his wrist. Lastly was a strip he cut from a tablecloth to create a makeshift scarf in order to hide his collar. With nothing more to do, he paced in front of the grandfather clock, his heart rate tripling when it neared the time to leave.

He made it down to the corridor with thirty seconds to spare. At exactly four o'clock, he peeked out of the door and looked both ways. Four guards stood in a cluster to the right, bantering and apparently in no particular hurry to get on with the change of staff. Gathering his courage and stiffening his spine, he slipped from the door and walked at a brisk pace in the other direction. Raw fear rang loudly in his ears, contending with the cacophony of the crowds until he feared he wouldn't be able to hear the stomping of boots chasing after him if he was discovered. He chanced a quick glance behind and almost stumbled with relief when he saw nothing except the lazy milling of vendors and buyers.

Squaring his shoulders with a new edge of confidence, he skirted around tables and stalls with his head held high and eyes low, for once in his life appreciative of his slight frame as he weaved easily in and out of the crowds. It was a lot busier than his previous visit but hardly a person batted their eye in his direction.

He saw it then.

A column sporting a red flag with the picture of a hammer and anvil on it toward the open doors, and near it a rusted, old pickup parked alongside the front wall just five yards from the entrance. It had a hunter green tarp covering the back that was tied with rope on both sides. Next to the doors were a series of garage doors that he assumed enabled the vendors to conveniently pack and unpack their wares each day. He approached the vehicle from the back and slowly made his way forward. Taking his only option, he glanced around, lowered the tailgate and scrambled inside. There was no choice but to slam it closed so the latch would catch and he waited with bated breath for the angry shouts of the owner, guards, anyone.

In the near darkness, he couldn't tear his eyes away from the inside of the tailgate, expecting at any second for it to be ripped open and for men to haul him out. Finally, after what seemed an eternity, the truck rumbled to life and jolted backwards. A minute later, it turned around then jerked forward to assume a steady, smooth rhythm. Corin checked the watch on his wrist constantly and waited for thirty minutes to pass before breathing a sigh of relief and turning to inspect the contents of the truck bed. It appeared to be filled with large sacks of grain and a few garden variety tools.

He found a narrow toolbox and searched within, grabbing a screwdriver and tucking it into his back pocket. Hardly an ideal weapon, but better than nothing. In his haste, he'd forgotten to pack a knife from the kitchen. An hour and a half later, the truck came to a stuttering halt, the engine sounding as if it had died rather than been turned off. The vehicle swayed a bit as he heard the driver get out and walk around to the back end. A voice raspy with old age greeted a man with a strong country accent. They exchanged information briefly then walked away until Corin could no longer hear them.

After picking up his bag, he lifted the tarp just enough to confirm he was alone, reached his hand out and released the latch to the tailgate. He climbed out, slammed the door closed and took off as quickly as he dared, heading to the side of the building he was close to. Against the wall with no one else in sight, he took a minute to gain his bearings.

The building turned out to be a gas station that had seen better days. The pumps weren't as advanced as those of the gas station a half-mile down the road from the hotel, but the premises was well kept. It seemed to be located on the outskirts of Wyntessen with miles of open desert in every direction. To the right lay the nearest signs of civilization and to the left was a flat horizon broken only by gently rolling hills that could be as far out as the neighboring territory for all the distance that appeared to be between him and them.

He knew Carnasess, the district that the central city was located in, was toward the hills. If memory served, there should be a road nearby that led south to Dubrough, his home district. The only trouble was finding it. He resituated the cloth around his neck, strapped the bag over his shoulder and walked around to the entrance of the building. Inside were rows of convenience items, both edible and non, with coolers at the back wall and a small coffee station to the side. His mouth watered at the sight. Damn, it'd been a while since he'd been allowed caffeine.

"Where the hell'd you come from, boy?"

Corin started, turning to find two older men several feet to his right. One stood behind the cashier counter and the other was leaning an elbow on it, obviously the truck driver since there was no one else in the store. He looked to the clerk, remembering to meet his gaze like a free man at the last moment, and attempted a smile.

"I'm traveling through."

"I didn't see no one on the road as I pulled up," the driver commented with narrowed, rheumy eyes.

"I...came from town," he lied. "I was wondering if you could point me toward the road that goes to Dubrough."

The clerk shifted a toothpick between his lips and put one hand out, palm up. "Sure, for five bucks."

Corin looked at the hand, feeling his stomach sink. "I-I don't have any money."

Both men erupted into loud gales of laughter, holding their paunches as though they couldn't contain their mirth. "I'm just playin' with ya, son," the clerk said while wiping his eyes. "Don't get much cause for humor 'round here what with the economy 'n all. Why you headed to Dubrough?"

"Family," he supplied, which was the truth.

"You walkin'?" the driver asked.

"Yes, sir."

Both men stared at him, as if trying to discern whether he was joking or not.

"You know that's 'bout an hour drive from here, right?"

Corin shrugged and nodded.

The driver grunted and hefted his weight from the counter. "Well, the road goin' there's 'bout three miles from town, which is where I'm headin'. Gimme five minutes to get some supplies and I'll drive you." He barreled off toward the coffee station without waiting for an answer.

Corin felt a grin play on his lips, not missing the irony of getting a ride from the man he'd been secretly traveling with for the past two hours.

"Grab some water."

He looked over at the clerk with a frown. "I'm sorry?"

The man jerked his head in the direction of the coolers. "Grab a bottle. No one needs to find some kid on the side o' the road dead from dehydration."

"But I can't—"

"Ain't no charge, boy. Now mind your elders and go on," the clerk said gruffly.

Corin paused, shocked by the generosity of both men, then did as he was told. He went for the smallest size, but stopped at a loud harrumph. The driver tapped the glass door Corin was holding as he made his way to the counter. "Big one, boy. Don't skimp on a good deed. They're too rare these days."

Switching bottles for a larger one, he went back to the counter and held it up for the clerk to see. The man nodded with a half-smile and rang up the driver's purchases. Before leaving, Corin thanked the clerk, who only nodded and went back to his work.

Three miles down the road, the driver let him out and pointed south. "Keep goin' that way till you come to a fork in the road. Head east and it won't be but twenty more miles till you get to Dubrough. Good luck, kid."

"Thanks." He got out and watched the man drive away before setting out on his journey. With only flatlands surrounding him, there was no point in walking at a distance from the road, but he felt the exposure keenly. His only hope to avoid being seen should Markus take this road to search for him was to lie down and try to blend in with the atmosphere. After an hour of stretching his neck to continuously glance at the road behind, however, he gave up and relied on his hearing to warn him of any coming cars.

The hot sun baked his skin through the extra material of the sweatshirt he didn't dare take off, not wanting to chance someone recognizing his platinum hair. It was a rare attribute among the people of his territory, which gave him good reason to keep it hidden. As the sun set over the western horizon, the discomfort in his backside began to shift from a dull ache to a cumbersome, piercing throb. It took all that he had to resist the urge to stop and rest by the side of the road. The sooner he reached the hotel, the sooner he could convince Madeline to take Amy and run with him across the territory line and start a new life.

He could find something with which to remove the hated collar around his neck and claim himself a free man where no one would know the difference. Money would only be an issue for a short time until he made enough to rent an apartment and find a real job. Meanwhile, he would do what he'd been trained to do and service others, trading his body for cash. Madeline was sure to be outraged once she found out, but she would eventually come to understand that it was necessary, just as he did.

Corin stopped long enough to pull out a hunk of French bread to eat then stuck his hands in his pockets when he was done. The temperature was rapidly decreasing and a chill set into his bones that slowed his pace even further. He hunched his shoulders against the gusts of unfettered winds and allowed his mind to recede into a lethargic haze. All feeling had been leached from his face, fingers and toes by the unrelenting climate, taking with it his coordination and causing him to stumble more than walk through the sparse brush lining the road.

And so it was that he didn't notice the car coming up fast behind him until it was too late. Headlights seared his eyes when he turned to see the car drive past then pull over to the side of the road. As quickly as his frozen body would allow, he started to run from the vehicle until he heard the sharp call of a woman's voice.

"Hey, there. Need a ride?"

Corin hesitated and looked back, seeing an arm waving at him from the driver's side window. He stood still, contemplating the wisdom of taking the offer then decided he might as well. If she was sent by Markus, she'd catch him no matter where he ran. By the time he reached the car, however, he was almost certain she wasn't associated with the leader. It was highly doubtful his men would be driving an old, beat up Volvo to search for a wayward slave.

He walked around to the passenger side when he saw the door open and climbed in. The woman inside had the classic looks of a loving grandmother, with short wisps of silvery hair styled meticulously atop a round face with cheeks lined from habitual smiles. Even sitting, he could tell she was short, though that didn't take away from the benevolence she seemed to exude.

"What's your name, sweetie?"

Corin put his bag at his feet then strapped the seatbelt on while he thought of an answer. "J-Josh," he stuttered, cringing inwardly at the first name that'd popped into his mind.

"Well, Josh, my name's Sharon. Why...? Good Lord, you're shaking like a leaf." She put the heater on to full blast then smacked his hands away when he tried to warm them. "Not there, honey, they'll heat up too fast. Put them under your shirt and around your chest. That's it. So, why were you headed off in such a rush when you saw me coming?"

He leaned into the flow of warm air, wincing at the sting in his thawing face, and spoke again once his lips were capable of forming words. "I j-just didn't want to get run over. Not sure if you would see me in time."

Her only reaction was the purse of her lips at the obvious lie. "Where you headed, sweetheart?"

"Dubrough."

"Well, you're in luck. I'm passing through there, so I can drop you off. I'd ask you to keep me awake, but you look like you're about to pass out. Go on and lean the seat back. The lever's on the side. I'll wake you when we get there."

"Thanks," Corin said with a hint of awe, somewhat staggered by his good fortune. It was almost too good to be true that he should run into three generous people willing to help. It boosted his spirits and gave him confidence that he might actually pull off his goal. Leaning the chair back, he dozed off and on for the rest of the trip, too excited to fully succumb to exhaustion. Forty minutes later, he awoke to a slight nudge to his elbow.

"Rise and shine, honey. We're here."

He stretched and blinked blearily at the scenery outside. They were passing through what must've been the town closest to the hotel, though he'd never been in it.

"Where do you want me to drop you off?"

He scrubbed the sleep from his eyes and looked at the elderly woman. "Are we on the west side of town?"

"About to be. My turnoff's just on the outskirts. That a good spot?"

"Yeah. Perfect." His luck held true when Sharon pulled into the gas station closest to the hotel for fuel. "I'm just half a mile up the road. I can get out here."

Sharon nodded and parked the car, a smile lifting the corners of her mouth. She grabbed his arm just as he was leaving and gave him a studious look. "Don't run, sweetie. It's like waving a red flag in front of a bull."

"Excuse me?" He flinched when she reached out and flicked the hidden collar at his neck before he could pull away.

"I've seen a lot of runaway slaves get snatched up simply because they got spooked and ran, thinking it was their Master. Walk like a free man with your chin held high till you can get that thing off. It's your only chance."

His breath hitched as he stared into her kind eyes, containing not an ounce of censure. Swallowing repeatedly, he finally got his throat to work and whispered, "Thank you."

Sharon nodded and placed a hand on his knee. "We all need a little help every now and then. I'm glad I was here for you. Now, go on, and remember what I said."

"Yes, ma'am." He smiled and got out, turning toward his destination. Fifteen minutes later, dawning light cast shadows on the one-story building that had been his home for his entire life. He veered from the road and angled a path to the back, feeling a sliver of dread take root in his gut as he neared.

It was eerily quiet, even for the early hour, and the parking lot was strangely empty. All the lights were turned off, including the ones underneath the overhang in front, and the plexiglass to one of the front doors was missing. Corin circled around back to the shed and found it unlocked. Tendrils of alarm clutched at his chest when he found the inside barren. Everything was gone, even the tattered mattress he'd slept on. Running to the back entrance, he saw that the key card mechanism was crushed and hanging from its wires, the handle to the door on the ground a few feet away.

He dropped his bag, opened the door and crept into the hallway, only to find there was no cause for stealth. All the doors to the rooms were either hanging from loose hinges or completely taken off. A quick survey around one room revealed the evidence of vandalism. Windows shattered, furniture gone or in ruins, dried mud caked to the carpet. He shook his head and backed out, flying to the room his sisters shared. It too was in the same state of abandonment with not a scrap of their belongings to be found.

Corin ran to the front desk next and found it and the office in shambles. All but the countertops had been stolen or damaged beyond repair. Not even the industrial-sized washer and dryer remained. It was as if the place had been deserted for years, its only redeeming value now that of providing a roof over the heads of transients.

Frantically, he searched through the clutter in every corner and room in an effort to find clues as to where his sisters had gone, unwilling to entertain the idea that he was too late. Sometime in the late afternoon, a thick web of despair fell over his thoughts and suppressed the functions of his brain. He staggered on autopilot to the back door to retrieve his bag then returned to the front desk. Back to the partition, he slid down to the floor, barely noticing the pain of his bruises. He stared at nothing. At everything. At the dreams in his heart that crumbled, one by one, into an abyss that swallowed them whole.

They were gone. His reasons for existing. The sisters he had sworn to protect and failed. He should've acted sooner, like Madeline had chastised him about before he'd been sold. He should've tried harder, killed his stepfather. *Something!*

Oh, God, please take this away. Take it all away, he begged, but no one answered.

Corin shouted, buried his face in his hands and wept.

Chapter Ten

A noise. Low, vibrating, annoyingly persistent. Then it was gone. Time passed, disturbed yet again by another sound. Like the muffled beats of a drum. It tugged at Corin's conscious and urged him to wake, but that was no easy task. A painful, wretched weight had settled into his bones and trapped his mind, holding him to the darkness where there was no emotion. No thought. The sound drew closer, intruding upon his solitude and stealing him into wakefulness.

Corin blinked open sore lids and looked up from his position on the floor. The form of a giant stood over him, lit up by the flood of headlights through the curtainless, cracked windows at Corin's back. He frowned in confusion, his brain not yet caught up with the vision his eyes took in.

Then it clicked.

Panic went into overdrive and he slapped at his back pockets in search of the screwdriver he'd stolen that was no longer there. He cast a cursory glance at the floor around him but came up empty. Markus strode purposefully toward him and he grabbed the only weapon at his disposal. Just as the man reached down, he brought up a long, jagged shard of glass in a vicious swipe, feeling it drag as it sliced through material and the skin of Markus' midsection. A loud curse rang out followed by a chorus of alarmed voices somewhere in the distance.

Sheer terror gave him strength and he jumped onto the desk in an attempt to get away. The leader's massive body collided into him from behind and propelled him forward, yet he landed on corded muscles instead of the hard, linoleum floor. In the next instant, he was rolled onto his back and straddled about the waist. Markus pinned his wrists to the floor and slammed the hand that held the shard onto the tile over and over again until it lost feeling and the glass fell free.

"Enough!" Markus roared.

But it wasn't. Corin fought like a madman to break the leader's hold, kicking with his knees and bucking his hips to no avail. The man atop him was more than twice his size and built like a steamroller, with iron fists that cut off the blood to his hands. Futility burst through his initial panic and the adrenaline-fueled energy that had surged through his system quickly began to dissipate. Hot tears gathered in his eyes and spilled over as a growl ripped through his chest.

"Let me go," Corin rasped.

Markus' dark gaze bore into him with strict determination. "You will stop fighting me immediately."

"I will never stop!" he yelled, bucking once more to hammer in his point. "It's because of you they're gone. You took me from them and put them in danger. I'll kill you before I s-stop looking for them." The last sentence ended on a sob that broke past his control. He should've been afraid, should've recanted the threat as soon as it was out, but he wouldn't. He meant it as surely as he knew the sun would rise on the morn, and nothing could change that fact.

They stared at each other for long seconds, Corin with a heated glare through tear-filled eyes and Markus with a hard, unreadable expression.

Without looking away, Markus said, "Parland, tell James to find 1048 East Pickard Road on the map. We have a few packages to pick up from there." He stood abruptly, pulling Corin with him in one fluid movement.

Corin struggled with everything he had left as Markus' huge arms trapped his own to his sides and lifted him with infuriating ease. He would not go back to the misery of his prison while his sisters were still out there, unprotected and vulnerable. Markus' firm grip on his jaw forced him to look at a man standing in front of them with a syringe half full of clear liquid.

"Calm down or I will sedate you. Understand?" Markus asked in a voice made all the more potent for its low tone.

Uncaring of his dignity, Corin resorted to frantic pleas, pushing rational into his scattered thoughts. "P-please, let me go. You don't need me anymore."

Markus snorted as he started for the entrance.

"I told you everything I know about your enemy. There's no reason to keep me. I swear I'll pay you back every cent of Scott's debt to you. J-just please…" Another sob came out when he saw the same Hummer that had driven him away the last time awaiting them with another man holding the back door open. A sea of anguish washed over him as he was carried inside and held tightly against Markus' chest, made to sit between his thighs. He dropped his head back to the leader's shoulder and bit his tongue to keep his teeth from chattering. When the vehicle rolled into motion, he made one last attempt to struggle, but it was over almost before it began, his nerves shot to hell and back.

Utterly drained with the black hole of his despair spanning out before him, he swiveled his gaze to the side and got lost in the scenery flying by. There was a distant, sharp pang in one of his hands as a strip of cloth was knotted around it, but he couldn't summon the interest to care. When the Hummer came to a stop and Markus pulled him out to guide him on numb legs, he was barely aware of his surroundings. At the arched doorway of a small mansion, one of Markus' men knocked and a minute later, a tall man with hawkish features and greying hair opened it. He was dressed in rumpled silk pajamas covered by a padded red robe patterned with gold paisleys that lay slightly off balance on his narrow shoulders as if he'd dressed in a hurry, yet his hair was immaculate.

"Can I help you?" the man asked in a tone dripping with condescension.

An irrational bout of laughter bubbled up in Corin's chest. That was the wrong attitude to take with a pissed off leader.

"Yes. I'm Markus Hammond and you have two things that I want."

The older man's eyes widened, darting over the six men at Markus' sides then out to the three vehicles invading his front lawn. "What trick is this?" he demanded imperiously.

The guard who'd knocked pulled out a gun and pointed it directly at the other man's forehead. "One that'll see you dead if you don't get out of the way."

The sight of the gun snapped Corin out of his daze as quickly as it caused the older man to jump aside.

"Relax, John," Markus said with deceptive coolness. "We'll be gone as soon as we have what we came for." He strode inside as if he owned the place, retaining possession of Corin by a firm hand on his wrist. John followed nervously after them, sputtering words of inquiry that somehow managed to sound respectful and haughty at the same time.

They passed through an immense foyer with a wide, curving staircase at the back and a huge crystal chandelier hanging above their heads. Thick, gold-plated frames holding gaudy works of art and plastic floral arrangements set on painted furniture appeared to be lavishly expensive, but lent not an ounce of warmth to the interior. The sitting room they entered to the left was decorated in much the same fashion, its color scheme matching that of John's robe and lit by soft lights and a flickering fire on the far end.

Corin took this all in fleetingly before his attention was drawn to the people that occupied the excessively furnished room.

Doreen looked a shadow of her former self and decades older than the fifty-one years she claimed. Her light blonde hair hung in strings around a face that was sunken in at the cheeks and eyes. She was curled up on the corner of a loveseat with a brandy glass full of golden liquor in one bony hand. Dull eyes sparked to life when she saw them, but they contained only a wealth of wariness.

To the right and crouched down at the side of a wide bookcase against the wall was Madeline. Instead of her usual snug jeans and button up blouse, she was wearing a white, flowing gown that fit her blossoming chest a little too well. Her chestnut hair was pulled back into a mussed braid, which exposed colorful bruises along the side of her face that Corin could see. Held tightly in her lap was Amy, who was dressed in nightwear befitting her age and displaying the same wide-eyed expression of fright as her sister. Her loose curls tumbled around her cherubic face, which was stained with tear tracks but blessedly free of bruises.

"Cory!" Amy exclaimed. When she tried to get to him, however, she was held down. Madeline's wild brown eyes flew from him to the rest of the men in the room before finally settling on John with no little amount of fear.

Corin knew that look. The trepidatious behavior of a person afraid to run to safety. That fearful uncertainty that could only come from abuse or neglect. From the evidence on her face and the lack of bruises on Doreen's, Corin knew that it was from both.

Fury surged to the forefront of his thoughts and he lunged at John, only to be restrained by the leader's arm banded around his chest. "You bastard!" he shouted. "How could you? I'll—"

"Stop!" Markus hissed in his ear. He blocked the sight of John with his larger frame and rattled Corin by the shoulders. "You will obey me. Is that clear?"

Corin's chest heaved with outrage, his body shaking, but he forced himself to surrender to his Master's command. There was a look of sheer determination in the man's eyes that told him a resolution would be found by his rules alone.

When Corin nodded almost imperceptibly, Markus curled one hand into the curve of his collar then turned to John. "How much do you want for them?"

John's mouth finally stopped flapping and he furrowed his brow. "The girls?"

"Yes. How much?"

The older man adopted a contemplative expression and opened his mouth for a response, but Doreen cut him off. She jumped up from the loveseat in righteous indignation and ran toward them, her drink spilling heedlessly to the plush carpet.

"You can't take my girls! They're mine!"

"You gave up full custodial rights when you divorced your ex-husband and married this man," Markus said coldly. "By law, he has as much right to them and interest in their welfare as you do. Therefore, if he feels they're being unfairly treated, he can sell them to someone more capable of providing for them—and that would be me."

Doreen stared in horror at Markus, mouth opening and closing in shocked silence. "But he's the one abusing them!" she screeched, jabbing a finger at John. "It's his fault."

Markus shrugged indifferently. "I wasn't here to witness that, so I can't take your word as truth."

The woman's face turned a brilliant shade of red and she sprang at him, her momentum swiftly interrupted by one of Markus' guards. The man pinned her arms to her sides and clamped her mouth shut with the palm of his hand. She writhed and kicked uselessly against his unyielding hold.

Markus turned back to John and lifted a brow.

John narrowed an avaricious gaze on Madeline and Amy, pinching his chin between a hooked forefinger and thumb. "They're both beauties and I haven't touched them yet, so they're still virgins."

Corin lunged forward again, not even realizing he'd moved until he was choked by the collar held in Markus' firm grip.

"I think one thousand for the both is a fair price."

"Five hundred," Markus countered, "and I won't tell your boss about the money you've been skimming from his revenues."

John's face paled significantly. "Fi-five hundred sounds good."

A humorless grin lifted the leader's lips. "I thought you might think so."

As if on cue, another of Markus' guards pulled a wallet from his back pocket and counted out the agreed upon bills, while a second went to collect the purchase. Madeline's eyes bulged at the man coming at her, but she seemed to regain a measure of composure and stood, pulling Amy up with her.

With one hand held up, palm out, she said, "Wait. Can we get our things?" Her voice shook only a little, which brought a swell of pride to Corin's chest. She'd always been mature for her age, and the courage she was showing now in the face of such adversity amazed him.

"You have five minutes," Markus granted.

It only took them three.

Madeline came rushing back with Amy on her heels, a small backpack slung over one shoulder and two large canvases in her hands. Corin knew them instantly, having stared at them nearly every night for years in the crowded shed that had been his bedroom. She handed them off to one of the men then looked at her mother. Doreen stilled and the man holding her released her mouth. The woman opened her arms as far as she could in invitation to her oldest daughter, her glistening eyes imploring more than welcoming.

"Come here, baby. Tell them you want to stay with me. Tell them it was John who was hurting you, not me."

Madeline's eyes welled up as her small hands curled into fists. "You *let* him hurt me! You did nothing while he—" Her sentence ended in a strangled sob, but she took a fortifying breath and pushed through, shaking her head sadly. "I love you, Mother."

As soon as Corin felt his Master's fingers retract from his collar, he gathered his sister's trembling body into his arms. She clung to him like a lifeline, drawing back long enough for him to pick up Amy and hold onto them both.

"Take them out to the car," Markus said, from somewhere behind them.

A hand at his back pushed him toward the front door and he went without hesitation. With a sister in each arm, he walked out of the mansion, leaving behind the tortured cries of their mother, and climbed into the backseat of the Hummer. Amy sat in his lap while Madeline curled up at his side and rested her face in the crook of his neck. Her breaths came in rapid, shuddering puffs, her sobs gradually increasing in volume until her body began to wrack with them. Corin wrapped an arm around her shoulders and drew her closer with a hand on her head. He rocked with whispered words meant to soothe, longing to take away her pain.

After a while, Markus sat down in the passenger seat and looked back at them as the driver started the vehicle and drove away.

"Where are we going?" Amy asked in a small voice.

Corin kept his gaze locked onto his Master's. "To a better place, I promise." An emotion flickered in the leader's eyes, but was gone before Corin could decipher it. Markus nodded once then turned around. Sometime later, Madeline fell into an exhausted sleep and Amy slid down to lie in her seat with her head on his thigh. Melodic songs from the CD in the disk driver filled the air during the trip and when they pulled up to the compound, it was to a side entrance he didn't recognize.

Gathering up Amy's tiny frame, he nudged Madeline awake and climbed out. Madeline stayed close as they entered the building with Markus leading them through a maze of halls similar to the path Heather had taken him down previously. When they came to the main corridor, all of them, including the six guards, took the elevator up to the eighth floor and got out.

Markus looked to one of his men, saying, "Put them in Brian's old room and make sure they have whatever they need."

"My pictures," Madeline spoke up belatedly. She reached out to take the canvases from the man carrying them but stopped when Markus placed a hand on them first.

"May I?"

Both Corin and Madeline frowned at the leader's request, knowing full well he had the authority to do whatever he wanted. Hesitantly, Madeline nodded and watched while Markus picked up one of the paintings to inspect it.

"How old were you when you did this?"

"Eleven," Madeline answered in a shy voice.

"This is very good," Markus remarked in a serious tone. He picked up the other and gave it a critical perusal. "I have an artist on site that I've commissioned to do several paintings for me over the next year or two. She's been looking for an apprentice to replace the last one she trained. The position is open if you want it."

Madeline gaped, with Corin quickly following suit. "You...you mean it? You'll really let me train with her?"

Markus frowned then said sternly, "I don't lie." He grunted, barely able to move the paintings in time before Madeline threw herself at him and hugged his waist. The perplexed, helpless expression on his face was so out of character, Corin felt a small smile curve his lips.

"Thank you. Oh my gosh, thank you! Cory, did you hear that? I'm going to be a painter!" She crashed into him next, narrowly missing her sister, who was beginning to rouse from the commotion.

"You *are* a painter," he reminded her. "Now take Amy and get some sleep. I'll see you tomorrow." A lump formed in his throat over the possibility that he might not. There was no telling what his punishment would be or whether it would be of a permanent nature. Reluctantly, he released Amy into her care and watched a guard take the canvases from Markus and walk them to a door in the middle of the hallway.

Markus dismissed the rest of his men then steered Corin by the collar up to the tenth floor and into the penthouse. "Strip," he ordered when they'd reached the bed.

Corin stared at the man's chin and waited for permission to speak. Fear of what was about to come sang persistently in his blood and slowly began to rise in tempo, but he was still too mystified by Markus' actions to give it lead. This would likely be his only chance to get answers to the burning questions in his mind and he was going to take it.

When Markus saw that he wasn't moving, he frowned and said, "Speak."

"How did you know where to find me, and where my sisters were and that my mother had divorced Scott? How did you know about John and that he was stealing from his company?" The questions he'd held in flew out in an uncontrollable rush, after which he sucked in his lost breath.

Markus' frown deepened and he sat on the bed with a sigh to take off his boots. "You're predictable. I knew you would try to find your sisters, so I left a few men near the hotel to notify me if you arrived while I searched every other district in the territory." He set aside his gun and knife and took off his clothes. There was an angry, red slash caked in dried blood across his upper abdomen from the shard Corin had used on him.

"I've been keeping track of your sisters since the day I bought you. Your mother divorced Scott just days later when she caught him trying to sell Madeline. She took the rest of their money, your sisters, and moved in with John. Scott abandoned the hotel after that and moved to the neighboring territory."

Markus walked over to Corin and began taking his clothes off, starting with the watch he'd stolen and the strip of material wrapped around his hand. Corin grimaced as the cuts on his palm he hadn't noticed before were stretched for inspection. "I'd already planned on getting them away from there, but you forced my hand early. After some research on John and discovering that he works for a man who works for me, it was a simple matter to find dirt on him to use to my advantage. Nobody can afford to be clean in this world."

Corin shivered, though whether it was from the words or the hands sliding up his ribs to take his shirt off, he didn't know.

"He's been taken care of, however. What your mother chooses to do now is up to her."

From the edge in his Master's voice and the smears of blood visible on his knuckles as he pulled Corin's shoes and pants off, Corin guessed he wasn't simply talking about the purchase of his sisters. He decided he could live without knowing what had happened to John after he'd left, although a part of him wished he'd been there to see it. His mind whirled at the implications of Markus' answers. After his Master pulled the rubber band from his hair, Corin placed a tentative hand on his forearm and stared at his chin. He had to know.

At his Master's nod, he asked, "Why?"

Markus lifted his jaw with two fingers so that their eyes met. "Because I know how important family is."

Corin held his breath speechlessly. This man was his enemy. A cruel Master who'd taken him from his loved ones and kept him for reasons unfathomable, using him every day in any way he liked. Yet the hatred he'd held onto dearly for so long wouldn't come. He felt lost in confusion without a solid anchor to hold onto. Nothing made sense anymore.

Markus took the cuffs from the nightstand, bound his wrists in front then led him by the collar to the center of the room. His height allowed him to reach the ceiling and unscrew what Corin had always assumed was the shade for a light that didn't work. A large metal hook dropped down, attached to a six-inch-long chain that was bolted to the ceiling. From an ornate chest near the piano, he pulled out the spreader bar, two carabiners and a much longer chain with a similar hook at one end and a padlock on the other. He looped the chain around the hook dangling from the ceiling and secured it with the padlock so that the second hook was hanging about a foot and a half above Corin's head.

Into this he looped the small chain, locking the cuffs together, stretching Corin's body until he was forced to stand on the balls of his feet to keep his balance. It was lost momentarily as Markus swept the rug out from underneath him to reveal two collapsible, iron rings bolted to the floor, approximately two feet apart. After strapping the spreader bar to Corin's ankles, he used the carabiners to lock the D rings on the leather straps to the iron rings in the floor.

By this time, Corin was breathing so rapidly he felt lightheaded. For the entire course of the trip back, the knowledge of his punishment had been a distant thought, easily shoved to a corner of his mind where he wouldn't have to dwell on it. Now that he was no longer able to push it aside, he found he wasn't nearly as prepared as he wanted to be. But then there never was a way to prepare for pain. There was only endurance, and the hope that it would end before it swallowed his sanity.

Sweat pricked Corin's brow as his Master left then came back around to his front, holding the cock ring. The device was put into one of his hands and his fingers were closed in a silent order to keep it until it was taken back. Markus skimmed his palms down Corin's torso then up again to pinch his nipples, teasing them into hard, little nubs. His fingers quested back down, tracing his ribs and burying themselves in the thatch of hair at his groin. Corin gasped as his flaccid cock was grasped in a firm grip that slowly began to nurse it to life. His body responded the way it was trained to do, blood hastening to fill his member as a wave of incited bliss rolled through him.

"Now it's my turn," Markus said in a low, almost seductive tone. "How did you escape?"

Corin's breath quickened even further, his mind scrambling to sort through which facts he could give away without divulging Mika's role. "I s-snuck out to the market when the guards weren't looking."

His Master stroked him from base to tip, adding pressure with his fingers to the underside. With his other hand, he cupped Corin's balls and began to massage the perineum behind them with the pads of his fingers. Corin groaned, letting his head fall back.

"Look at me," Markus commanded.

He raised his head and fixed his gaze on Markus' chin, still able to see the gleaming intent in his eyes.

"If you lie, I will make this last for hours."

Corin gulped audibly and shook his head. He knew exactly how painful it was to have an erection that was allowed no surcease from constant stimulation. "I'm n-not lying, Master. They were changing shifts and didn't see me."

"And then what?" He increased his strokes, tugging on his balls lightly and rolling them in his palm.

"I hid in the back of a truck and stole a ride to Wyntessen. Ahh!" The hand on his cock was pumping faster now, so tight that the friction flushed him with heat and heightened his arousal. "Then I w-walked to Dubrough. A lady gave me a ride halfway there."

"Who told you about the change of the guard?"

Corin's eyes widened despite his effort to hide his reaction. "N-no one." His Master began stroking him furiously, covering his entire length in a merciless grip and squeezing his balls. Sparks of pleasure lit Corin's skin afire and a tingling sensation raced down his spine. His orgasm was coming fast and he knew he'd be unable to prevent it. "Master!" Markus stopped suddenly, pinching just below the head and pulling down on his testicles. When the tip of the man's thumb dug forcibly into his slit, he cried out at the shock of pain.

"Who told you?" Markus repeated.

Corin pried open his clenched lids and saw through his lashes the fevered lust in his Master's eyes, but he knew from experience that the man had patience in volumes. This would only end when he was ready. Even so, Corin steadfastly refused to give up his partner in crime. "No one," he said again.

Markus went back to pumping lazily, enticing his cock to regain its lost rigidity. "So, I take it you're willing to accept Mika's punishment for her?"

His body stiffened in alarm as his gaze flew to meet Markus'. It was there. The calm certainty that the man was aware of everything. Why hadn't he seen it before?

Because he'd been so caught up in the control of his body that he'd seen only what his Master had wanted him to see. "Y-yes," he replied, willingly consigning himself to the unknown punishment.

Markus leaned down to press their foreheads together then lower still to brush his lips across Corin's in a featherlight touch. The kiss was tentative at first, incongruent with the sheer power his Master usually dominated him with and when it deepened, Corin fell into it unreservedly. The gentle strokes of the tongue guiding his were languorous and intimate, leading him in a slow dance that caused a yearning to build in his gut despite the situation.

When Markus pulled away, he whispered softly, "So be it."

The cock ring was taken from his hand and his member was once again brought to a raging swell.

Unable to rock his hips into the strong grip, he moaned in desperation, his orgasm racing swiftly to an inflamed peak. Markus' fingers clamped down on its urgency at the last moment and the cock ring was quickly strapped to his balls and base.

His Master walked around to his back and after a few seconds, brushed a hand softly down his spine. That was all the warning he had. The switch that had previously been used to get his attention, whipped across his shoulders, calling a seam of fire that blazed across his skin. Another landed before he could take a breath and he bit his lip to keep from crying out. In rapid succession, the switch landed across every inch of his back, delivering blistering pain that gradually mounted as the punishment wore on.

The strikes weren't hard enough to break the skin, but Corin couldn't help the scream that was eventually ripped from his throat. He cried out until his voice was hoarse and his muscles shook with the effort to arch away from the stinging agony. Though the force of the blows didn't lessen, the pain seemed to gradually alter to a tolerable ache that allowed his mind to rise above the feverish cloud that trapped it. Only this time, it didn't feel as if he were escaping the reality of the situation as he'd done so often in the past. Instead, the knowledge that it was Markus at his back, Markus whose temperate authority had never pushed him beyond what he could endure, brought forth a swell of trust he couldn't deny. This was a punishment, not a beating—a lesson rather than an attempt to break him.

The first lash across the bruised mounds of his ass tore through his concentration and pulled another scream from his sore throat. He sagged against his restraints, depleted of energy, and moaned faintly as a hand smoothed over the latest mark. Another lash came, followed by a ragged sob and his Master once more caressed the line of blazing heat until the pain became tolerable. This ritual was repeated three more times, each strike harder than the last and each caress more lingering, more soothing along his abraded skin.

Awareness slowly set in when arms wrapped around him and his Master pressed their bodies together. The friction of skin on his beaten flesh brought a fresh wave of agony, but all he could manage was a weak moan. Then Markus pulled away and an oiled finger slid over his puckered ring and pushed its way inside. A second was added and they speared in and out of his channel, coaxing his entrance to make way for something larger. After a third slipped in, they worked his hole with vigor, stretching him wide until the burning sting of his nerves began to fade. Then they hooked around and found the spot they were searching for.

Corin's head fell back, a whimper drawn from his lips as pleasure bloomed in his groin. He didn't think it was possible to feel anything other than the flames licking at his back, yet he couldn't deny his reaction. His cock throbbed painfully in its trap as more blood tried to fill it. When the fingers withdrew, hands clasped his hips and the flared head of his Master's thick cock pushed at his entrance to replace them. Instead of the careful, easy invasion it had taken before, it slammed into him with brutal force. Corin cried out as the blunt tip battered his insides, snaking into his gut and burying itself there over and over again.

When Markus shifted angles and Corin's pelvis was rocked back to meet each one of the hard thrusts, the head of the cock in his ass rubbed over that spot repeatedly. It built up a tide of pressure in Corin's balls that had no way out. Suddenly, his Master pulled away and bent down to release his ankles from the straps of the spreader bar. He was lifted by an arm around his chest, his cuffs taken from the hook and his limp body laid out over the bed. He hissed from the sting of the comforter on his pain-ridden back, too exhausted to find the energy to roll over.

Markus spread his legs wide to accommodate his large frame, bending Corin's knees to his chest and folding him in half. Corin's wrists were stretched high over his head and pushed into the mattress by the weight of the hand leaning on them.

"Look at me," Markus demanded in a voice laden with hunger.

The tip of Markus' cock bore down on his entrance and as soon as his eyes locked with his Master's, it thrust in to the hilt. Corin shouted as his body was shoved forward and he tried to summon the strength to keep his arms straight and reduce the friction of material scraping along his backside. Markus resumed his rigorous pace, plunging into Corin's depths without mercy. He took possession of Corin's mouth in an aggressive kiss, delving inside and enforcing his supremacy with the dominant swipes of his tongue.

When he pulled back, he growled, "Open your eyes."

Corin obeyed, fighting to keep them open when his Master fisted his swollen cock and began pumping it in rhythm with his thrusts. Tears leaked from his eyes as the pain and pleasure blurred together until they became one driving force that had him yearning for more.

"You will never run from me again, do you understand?"

Corin swallowed convulsively around whimpered pants, unable to get his voice to work. He thought he sensed a hint of desperation, of fear, underlying the man's tone, but was too caught up in the sensations riddling his body to concentrate. A storm built inside that pushed him to his limits, creating a need which compelled his hips and urged them to meet each of his Master's pummeling thrusts.

"Do you understand?" Markus repeated, driving himself harder and faster into Corin's sheath.

"Y-yes, Master," he whispered. Then his cock and balls were unfastened from their prison at the same time his Master growled the command to come. The explosion of his orgasm ripped through him with a fury that wrenched a rough cry from his throat and arched his back from the mattress. Markus slammed into him twice more and shouted his release, shooting his load deep into Corin's channel. The pulsing ecstasy combined with the pain was overwhelming and he couldn't stop the sobs that tore through his chest.

Markus slowly pulled out and wiped the tears from his cheeks, even as more replaced them. The man let go of his wrists and leaned forward, pressing their foreheads together and sighing into Corin's mouth.

"Enough. It's over now."

But Corin couldn't stop. Not until a hand wrapped securely, possessively, around his throat and his Master's mouth slanted over his. The kiss was in direct opposition to the fierceness he was still reeling from—gentle, tender, yet with a seductive insistence that urged him to respond rather than simply endure. The unexpected change was distracting as his tongue was maneuvered in a slow and confusing tangle and the knot of suffocating tension in his chest gradually unfurled. With the tension left every ounce of his strength and by the time Markus had finally pulled back, his body was nothing more than a drained shell, still trembling from the aftermath of sensations.

"Go to sleep," his Master ordered softly.

And he did.

Chapter Eleven

Chords of sweet sorrow floated through the air and crept into the recesses of his mind, luring him into wakefulness. Corin blinked open his eyes and took a moment to gain his bearings. He was alone in the bed and the diffused light seeping in through the gauze-covered windows marked the hour of twilight. Memories of the past two days came back to him with crystal clarity, though his body felt strangely dissociated — sluggishly resisting his attempts to move.

When he braced himself to sit up, a flash of metal at his wrists caught his attention. The leather cuffs he'd always worn to bed had been replaced by slim, flat bands of jet black onyx with small loops on the insides of his wrists connected by a thin carabiner. They were simplistically aesthetic and molded for comfort, preferable in every way to the leather cuffs, except for the fact that they appeared seamless. Permanent. Curiously, the idea wasn't nearly as upsetting as he thought it should be.

There was also a large pad of gauze taped over his left pectoral from a wound that stung now as he stretched. He wanted to remove the covering and look at it, having no idea of what might have caused it, but he had to find his Master first. He held his breath against the protest of sore muscles and stood, clutching at the headboard when a wave of dizziness swept over him. Carefully, he made his way to the source of music and found Markus sitting at the grand piano, his head bent and fingers gliding over the keys fluidly. No acknowledgment of his presence was made, and, reluctant to break the spell cast by the sweet notes, he sank to his knees beside the bench and listened to the haunting melody until it came to a mournful end, masterful yet somehow tragic in its beauty.

Markus turned and teased a strand of Corin's hair between his fingertips then ordered in a tired voice, "Go to the bathroom."

Corin glanced up before obeying, taking note of the bags under Markus' eyes and the slump of his shoulders, as if he hadn't slept in too long—perhaps not since the day Corin had left, if he'd really gone to every district in search of him. After relieving himself, he stared at his reflection in the mirror. Fine stubble tinted his jaw a shade darker than his pale skin and his entire backside was a colorful mass of raised welts and dark bruises. They looked exceedingly worse than they felt, however, and were merely marks instead of open lacerations. A far less severe punishment than what he deserved, considering the gravity of his crime and the threat to Markus' life he'd made in front of the man's personal guard.

Corin touched the pad on his chest, the temptation to find out what it was hiding frozen when his Master appeared behind him and placed a hand over his. Markus' face, clearly visible above his own, held an unreadable expression that softened the depths of his eyes. He reached his other hand around and grasped Corin's cock in an unyielding grip, pumping it in leisurely strokes and milking pearly drops of pre-cum from its weeping slit. Arresting tendrils of arousal flared instantly throughout Corin's body, called forth by that strong touch. He had no choice but to lean back into the man's solidity to keep his balance, the flash of pain only adding to the intensity. His member swelled and curved in rigidity, as it was flawlessly manipulated by the hand that wielded it.

When Markus began to remove the gauze, Corin peered through hooded lids at the stylized engraving that was revealed on his chest. Carved in old English were the letters MH, made with such fine incisions that it was as if someone had drawn them on with a fountain pen. His Master must have drugged and branded him with his initials sometime during the night, staking an irrefutable claim on his property that no one could contest—not with its uniqueness. Corin had seen scarification before, but nothing that had been this terrifyingly beautiful.

Markus ran his fingers lightly over his mark, saying in a low, dominating voice, "You're mine." He continued to handle his slave's engorged shaft for a few seconds longer then squeezed its base before releasing it. "But I have a problem."

Corin dug his nails into his palms in an effort to keep from fisting his aching erection, as Markus started the shower and guided him in.

"I now have two additional slaves of an inappropriate age for a military compound," Markus said, while he poured soap onto his loofa and began to wash his body. "However, I have a feeling that if I were to send them away, my boy would chase after them, no matter how many times I beat him." He lifted a meaningful brow at Corin, whose cheeks flushed with heat at the truth. "Therefore, I have assigned a person I trust to be their caretaker. See to their education and watch over them every day. They will remain on the eighth floor, but you no longer have permission to leave this apartment without supervision. If you do, you can expect nothing less than what you were given last night."

Corin shuddered, in no way eager to relive that punishment. He looked to Markus' chin to ask when he would be allowed to see his sisters but was ignored. His Master washed his hair then switched the loofa for a washcloth and started on Corin's front.

"They will remain here until Madeline's of age, at which point she can take Amy and decide what to do from there."

"You'll release them?" Corin blurted out. It wasn't unusual for freemen enslaved to be released once they'd worked off their debt, but Markus had spoken of education, apprenticeship and a care provider, three things that would cost him money rather than gain it for him over the next three years. With a stern look from Markus, he bowed his head and turned around at the man's gesture. His cock was once more taken into hand and his arousal renewed with a surging rush. He put his hands on the wall as his Master pumped his flagged erection back to its pulsing thickness, caressing the ridges of the head with his calloused palm. Waves of pleasure crashed through him as the pace quickened and his hips began to buck into the enticing rhythm.

His fingers clawed at the wall when the washcloth slid over his enflamed skin, but the diversion of his Master's hand held most of the throbbing sting at bay. The torture at both sides continued until his entire backside was washed. However, it didn't stop there. When the cloth was dropped and Markus slowly inserted two fingers into his hole, he moaned at the burn of the intrusion. The bundled nerves at his entrance were still recovering from the force of the leader's rough urgency to discipline his slave. Even so, with the friction of the pulls on his straining member, his orgasm quickly spiraled beyond his control.

Markus leaned in and said gruffly, "I already have what I want." He increased the pressure of his hand and speared his fingers in and out, causing both pain and pleasure that pushed Corin unrelentingly toward the edge.

"Master!" he cried, his balls tightening in preparation to release their load, just as the hand on them tugged them down swiftly. He panted from the sudden cessation of his racing climax, lowering his head between his arms and trembling slightly.

An unexpected emotion began to seep in, replacing the lost rush of his climax. Something other than gratitude that stirred his blood and tightened his chest. And when his Master turned him to take his lips in a kiss, he wasn't satisfied to let it be a one-sided affair. He poured this new emotion into the heat of his Master's mouth, moaning softly when Markus' responding growl vibrated through him.

Markus broke away, breathing heavily and massaging his own stiff erection briefly. "Get ready. You'll have company soon."

Corin frowned at the cryptic words, watching silently while his Master removed the link binding his cuffs then got out and left the room with a towel in hand. After washing his hair and attending his hygiene, he found Markus standing by the bed, fully dressed and armed. From a tube, he smeared ointment onto Corin's brand, covered it with another thin pad then spread cream from a jar on the nightstand over his fresh welts. He nodded to a set of clothes laid out on the comforter and said, "Get dressed."

A knock on the door came before Corin could try for another question and he hurried into his outfit, wondering who his Master could be entertaining at— he glanced at the clock and saw that it was just past six—this early in the evening. Only Heather and the doctor ever came by, and Corin had no need of medical attention. After Corin had put his clothes on, Markus walked to the front and called out his command to admit the guest.

Corin followed him then stood, stunned, as Heather and his sisters blustered animatedly into the penthouse, holding numerous bags and other items.

"Cory!" Amy rushed over and curled her arms around his neck in a fierce hug when he bent to meet her. Bursting with excitement, she wriggled away and spread her arms wide, twirling in her new outfit. "Look what I got. I'm pretty! And my shoes," she said, pointing at her feet. Head to toe, she was the picture of a little girl happily spoiled. With black, shining shoes and white stockings topped by a strawberry-red dress trimmed in white frills, there was not a part of her that wasn't alive with vibrant color. Even her ribboned pigtails danced with merriment.

"You look very pretty," he affirmed with a smile.

"Amy," Heather called in a singsong tone.

"Oh!" She skipped to take a folded piece of paper from the woman's hand and headed off Markus just as he was stepping out of the door. Holding up the paper, she said, "I made this for you."

Markus paused and the room went silent while he opened the card to look at the picture Corin could vaguely see drawn in crayon from the other side. He'd never heard the man laugh, let alone seen a genuine smile lift his rugged features, so it came as no little shock when Markus knelt down on one knee and flashed his white teeth in appreciation.

"This is beautiful. Thank you."

Amy leaned in close and whispered conspiratorially in his ear. Whatever she said caused the leader to chuckle in a rich, deep bass that held Corin mesmerized. That a small child could strip the leader of their territory of his title and make him a mere man enjoying another's company was absolutely amazing. Not even around his men did he break his cool exterior with a hint of humor.

"I'll try to remember that," Markus said. "Now be good for Heather and do what she says, okay?" After Amy nodded eagerly, he lifted his gaze and the emotions in his eyes when they locked with Corin's were indescribable, yet infinitely compelling.

And gone in the next instant.

Corin didn't become aware he'd been staring at the door his Master had left through until Madeline pulled him into a crushing hug. He grunted at the spark of pain that lanced down his back before he could stop himself, causing his sister to jerk back in surprise.

He shrugged off her concerned frown and managed a smile. "I'm just sore—haven't been able to sleep much lately." She narrowed her eyes in disbelief, but he plowed on through the question he could see building in them. "You look great. Both of you do. Did you guys go shopping?" He couldn't get over the vast improvement that a set of new, *appropriate,* clothes made in the way Madeline looked from the night before. Or maybe it wasn't just the outfit. Maybe it was the relief of regaining the measure of safety that had been stolen from her, that Markus had provided for her and Amy because it was what his boy wanted. The thought sent another strange emotion flitting through his gut.

There were still ugly bruises marring one side of Madeline's face, but the rest of her was positively glowing.

"Of course we went shopping," she said, her worry disappearing as she glanced back at Heather with a smile. "Markus wouldn't give us a choice. He made his men take us out to the shops in the district and buy whatever we wanted. I got a full set of art supplies and Amy got a bike. Heather says we need to start on our school work as soon as our books come in, but we can come over here for dinner every night. Isn't that great? I had no idea the leader could be so nice."

Neither did I. Corin looked dazedly to Heather for confirmation and was met with a wide-toothed grin.

"Is he nice?" Madeline asked then, her tone altering subtly to one of uncertainty.

Corin's throat clogged and he cleared it twice before saying, "Yeah. He's a good man. I guess... I just didn't see it at first."

Madeline searched his eyes and apparently found whatever she was looking for when she nodded faintly and gave him a light kiss. Over the next few hours, the girls cooked, ate and joked, trying to include him as much as possible, but he couldn't quite bring himself to focus on their conversation. Markus' generosity came with a price—Corin's freedom, his body, his promise to stay when he might otherwise try to leave again—yet those sacrifices didn't hold as much significance as they once had. His Master wanted only him, and had gone to great lengths to keep him as well as make him happy.

Was it such a terrible thing to be coveted so profoundly? To surrender himself to a man who'd turned out to be more decent than any of the men who had used him before in his lifetime?

"That's his father," Heather said quietly.

Corin jumped, not realizing that his friend had come to stand beside him, or that he'd been staring at the picture on the wall opposite the table of the man who greatly resembled Markus. The sounds of his sisters' laughter rang out in the background, letting him know they were still engaged in their game of pool.

"Does he...?" Corin hesitated on the question he'd always yearned to ask. "Does he know what kind of man his son is?"

Heather sighed and stared at the photograph with him. "No. He only knew what kind of man he was." At Corin's inquisitive glance, her voice took on a low, sad cadence. "When I started as Master's housekeeper, I was so afraid of him because he never showed emotion. I thought him a monster, probably like you did, until someone who knew of his past took pity on me and explained why he's so distanced." Taking a deep breath, she continued, "The late Mr Hammond, his wife and four out of five of their children were murdered by the last leader who ruled over our territory and a group of his men. Supposedly, it was because Mr Hammond refused to donate his riches to a leader he thought would use his money unwisely.

"Master had been a police officer at the time and away on duty. When he came home a week later, it was to find his family slaughtered and their money seized. He was so furious, he went to the leader and threatened his life. It was a challenge that could only end in death and so he became the new leader."

Corin saw his Master's face in the picture of the man before him, taking in the minute differences between them that he hadn't noticed before, like the set of their jaws and the lines creasing their faces. The late Mr Hammond looked happy in the photograph, utterly at odds with his Master's disposition. What must it have been like for him to lose everything he'd held dear? Corin had lost his sisters, but not to something as permanent as death.

"I've threatened him twice," he whispered absently, remembering the first time and the strange look in Markus' eyes, almost as if the leader had admired him for it.

"Another slave told me once," Heather started, "that it is not we who depend on our Masters, but rather it is our Masters who depend on us. For whatever reasons, Markus needs you, and you need him — even if your reasons aren't the same."

Corin looked at her sharply, surprised to hear their Master's name on her lips. It somehow made the man more human, just as her words seemed to drive home a point he'd already suspected.

"I need you, too," Heather said softly, gaze averted as if the admission had cost her.

He was about to ask what she meant, when a loud, exultant shout from Amy shattered the moment and brought them back to their surroundings.

"I won, I won!" Amy cried, as she barreled around the corner and ran straight for her new caretaker.

Heather swept her up in a spinning hug and showered down affectionate praises, her face alight with joy and contentment. At that moment, the meaning of Heather's words dawned on him. The love of Heather's life and her only child were lost as surely as Markus' family was, and whether Amy and Madeline knew it or not, they were well on their way to replacing that empty space Corin had glimpsed in the woman on occasion. At the same time, his sisters were gaining the kind of motherly provider they deserved—one that wouldn't cower at the bottom of a snifter when their welfare was at risk.

And all of it was contingent upon his submission to his Master. Though once he would've looked on that as an unfair trade, Corin had to admit he no longer saw his submission as a sacrifice. Not when his Master was so willing to meet him halfway.

They all contributed to cleaning up, and when they were done, he kissed his sisters goodnight then asked them to wait outside with the door propped open while he spoke to Heather. Pulling his friend to the side where they couldn't be overheard, he said, "When they were still at the hotel, my stepfather... He..."

"Tried to prostitute Madeline," Heather supplied. "Master told me. Poor thing. Sick fucker!" she ground out.

Her attitude flipped so suddenly Corin raised his brows in shock.

"Well, he is! What kind of pathetic jerk could do that to his own child?" She widened her eyes in horror. "Oh, Corin, I'm sorry. I didn't mean—"

"It's okay," he said with a shrug. He'd been so young when Scott had started selling him, he'd readily accepted it as the norm, just as he had his abuse. Madeline, on the other hand, had never been used against her will, and he feared she might have lasting repercussions from the threat of her father.

The sympathy that flashed in Heather's blue eyes was quickly masked with her usual grace, for which he was thankful. "Don't worry, I'll talk to her. Master moved me into the apartment next to hers, so I'll always be close. Oh, and he told me to tell you he's meeting with a dignitary tonight. Apparently a guy named Craig — the youngest son of the leader we're warring with — came to negotiate a deal, so there's no telling when he'll be back. He also said to make sure you're in bed when he returns and not to wait up for him."

"Why didn't he tell me?"

Heather quirked one corner of her mouth. "I think he wanted this to be a surprise," she said, waving a finger to indicate herself and his sisters waiting in the hall.

Corin nodded and smiled appreciatively. When the girls were gone, however, sleep was the last thing on his mind. His thoughts raced with all he'd learned about his Master and the questions still broiling in his mind. That Markus truly understood the importance of family, he knew now, but that didn't account for the man's charity. Corin was his possession, and so, too, were Amy and Madeline now. He could keep them all as slaves for as long as he wanted, yet he only wanted his boy. The concept of such kindness was still too difficult to wrap his head around.

He stripped out of his clothes and put them in the laundry basket then knelt in front of the door. He would wait, and when his Master came, he would ask why the man was showing unnecessary kindness. Why he'd chosen a damaged boy to trouble himself with and what his ulterior motive was. There had to be one other than keeping a slave that was already his to begin with.

He must have dozed off at some point for the next thing he knew, Markus' strong arms were lifting him from the floor and carrying him to the bed. Corin stared at his Master's chin as his cuffs were linked together, trying to clear the fog of sleep from his mind to formulate his questions then he noticed the increased haggardness of the man's features—the dull look in his eyes and the weary bow of his spine.

"Didn't Heather tell you to wait for me in bed?" Markus asked.

Fencing in his impatience, Corin replied, "Yes, Master, but I wanted to talk to you."

Markus put away his weapons and clothes then climbed into bed. "Whatever it is, it can wait for the morning. Go to sleep." He situated the covers on top of them then pulled his slave close.

When Corin squirmed at the discomfort of coarse hair scratching the welts on his backside, he received a smart smack on the ass, but was rolled over onto Markus' chest, his head resting on his abdomen. He lay there for a while, storing his inquiries for the suspended conversation in the back of his mind then closed his eyes and obeyed his Master.

Chapter Twelve

There was no opportunity to speak about his issues in the morning, or even to service his Master in the usual routine he'd expected to resume upon his capture. Instead, Markus delivered ten powerful swats to his behind hard enough to bring tears to his eyes for disregarding the relayed command to get into bed early last night. The sting was rubbed away soothingly afterwards, while he was given instructions for the day.

When Markus mentioned that a guard would be posted outside of the penthouse door while he was gone, Corin forgot himself and blurted out, "I won't run again. My sisters are here."

Markus sat him up on the bed and feathered a thumb wordlessly over his bottom lip. His eyes were shaded with the same indefinable emotion Corin had seen before and he wondered again at the man's motives for his actions. There was a depth to his secretive gaze that reminded Corin of the tragic loss of his Master's family. A thought came to mind that was both disturbing and, in a way that he couldn't deny, saddening. For whatever reason, Markus had chosen him for a personal slave, and perhaps the lengths he'd taken to make that slave happy beyond normal reasoning and expectations spoke of a tenacity born of personal suffering.

Could Markus have done what he did in an effort to keep from losing one more thing he valued in his life? The idea that Corin could hold that much importance to a man he'd initially thought incapable of mercy caused his stomach to flutter. He'd never been looked upon by another man as anything more than a fuck toy, as Heather had so elegantly put it, yet what Markus had done for him made him feel otherwise. It made him feel...wanted, not simply possessed.

When Markus headed for the front door to leave, Corin hesitated in indecision, knowing he would probably get punished for speaking without permission twice, yet needing to say something. "Master," he called out. Markus turned in the doorway to look at him with brows furrowed. "I... Thank you. For saving my sisters and...everything." It wasn't enough—not by a long shot—but his throat tightened on the sincerity of his words.

Another unreadable emotion flitted across Markus' face and he nodded once then was gone. Corin started on his chores, distracted from his tumultuous thoughts only when Heather came to escort him to the laundry room and pantry. Amy was with her, waiting on her school books to arrive by mail to start her tutoring and Madeline was already training with her art instructor. The guard Markus had posted at the door accompanied them at a distance with a bored expression while they completed his tasks. Back at the penthouse, Corin bid them goodbye then kept himself busy until they met him again for dinner that night.

It was strange yet exhilarating to be able to eat and laugh with his sisters together at a table. He couldn't manage more than a smile at first, expecting at any moment for Scott to appear and beat him for daring to think that he was part of the family, or for Markus to demand that he kneel at his feet. Eventually, the good humor of his friend and sisters overrode his nervousness and he learned to relax. Markus didn't return until past midnight and passed out from exhaustion as soon as he crawled into bed.

The next three days passed in the same manner. His Master was becoming increasingly agitated by the negotiations taking up the majority of his time, but the leader never laid a harsh hand on him to vent his anger. Indeed, he hadn't been used at all or even touched, except for his Master's unyielding embrace at night, his gentle caresses and pleasure-inducing stimulations that always left Corin unbalanced and craving more.

It was on the fourth day that he received a call from Heather over the intercom by the bed in the late morning.

"Corin. Corin, you there?"

He hurried to the small, silver plate affixed to the wall and held down the button like he'd seen his Master do. "Heather?"

"Yeah. I'm taking the girls into town to see a dentist. Their appointment wasn't until next week, but the doctor had a cancellation and was able to fit them in today. I gave you the spot for next week."

Corin frowned. Markus had arranged for his sisters to see a dentist? *And* him? Somehow, it wasn't as much of a surprise as he thought it might've been, not anymore. Still, it made him pause in wonder.

"We'll be back in time for dinner, but I won't be able to go with you to do your chores. The guard will have to take you. Just let him know when you're ready. He should've already been notified of the situation."

"Okay. I'll see you at dinner then."

"Yup. Gotta go now before Amy loses her nerve and I have to drag her out of here. She's a little scared."

Corin's heart clenched at being unable to go with them. "Tell her a story—one with princesses and fairies. It'll help to calm her." When Heather laughed, Amy piped up in the background and insisted on his suggestion. It brought a grin to his lips, despite the ache in his chest.

"All right, I guess so," Heather said dramatically. "Boy, the things I go through." The love in her voice was obvious and belied her delight in doing something even so trivial as telling a story to one of her new charges.

He finished cleaning the kitchen then got dressed to go out, deciding to wait until he came back to eat lunch. With the laundry basket in hand, he opened the door with his voice command and nodded to the guard. Just as he stepped through, the elevator doors at the other end of the hall opened to emit five men Corin had never seen before, plus one that was all too familiar. Josh trailed behind the group with a faint smile and a glint of vindication in his eyes that sent a chill of foreboding down Corin's spine.

The men were dressed similarly in black attire with light jackets on, but it was the man in front that held Corin's attention. He carried himself with an air of supremacy and strode forward with grim purpose. Before Corin could react, the man leading the group withdrew a gun from a harness at his side, aimed and pulled the trigger. The guard standing obliviously at the door stiffened and his chest punched outward a heartbeat before he toppled ungracefully to the floor. Corin stumbled back in terror, dropping the basket and tearing his gaze from the man as the group advanced on him with deadly intent.

It wasn't until they were halfway down the hall that he remembered how to move and raced to the intercom beside the bed. Pressing the button with a trembling finger, he shouted, "Heather! Get Master. Heather —" He flinched back when the plate exploded in a shower of sparks as a bullet blasted through the wiring inside. Spinning around, he felt adrenaline surge in a nauseating rush at the sight of the men spreading out in the middle of the room to block off his only exit. Not that he could have outrun them. He was tempted to close himself in the bathroom, but there was no lock on the door and it was no protection against a gun.

The man returning his gun to its holster was of medium build, taller than the others with a shaved head that accentuated his austere features and the cruel set to his thin lips. He tilted his head to the side to indicate someone behind him and ordered, "Come here, slave."

Josh, who appeared slightly shaken now, shuffled forward.

"Is this him?"

"Y-yes," Josh confirmed. "That's my Master's new boy."

The man in charge backhanded Josh across the face, sending him spiraling to the floor. "I'm your Master now, you sniveling brat. If I hear you give anyone else my title again, I'll leave you here in the miserable life you begged me to take you away from. Do you hear me?"

"Yes, Master," Josh said as he shakily gained his feet.

The man turned back to Corin and appraised him with a rapacious, sweeping gaze. "So you're the one I've been hearing about. The boy my enemy covets so preciously. I have a proposition for you."

Corin took a small step back, not having felt the sense of being trapped so keenly since the last time Scott had cornered him in a fit of drunken rage.

"It seems as though your Master is being as unreasonable as ever. You see, he has this foolish notion that we can improve our economies by banding together and pooling our resources, which I'm in complete agreement with, but he wants to accomplish that by providing all slaves with the opportunity to work for their freedom. He thinks granting them their independence will motivate them to work harder and stay in the territory once they're free, thereby boosting our markets and allowing us to take advantage of some of the perks the richer territories enjoy. But he's wrong."

Corin froze as realization hit him. This must be the man Heather had told him about, the son of the leader of the neighboring territory. Greg... No, Craig was his name. More than that was the shock of the disdainful words spewing from his mouth. Was that really Markus' intention, to free the slaves and give them a chance to live and work for themselves as free members of society? A part of him could understand Craig's unwillingness to take that risk. Convincing the slaves to remain and safely build families of their own when for so long they'd been forbidden even that basic right would be tough—however, Corin also knew it was every slave's dream. It would increase the population, which might eventually give them enough people to facilitate luxuries like cellphone companies and more hands to farm the lands, bringing new business to the area.

"Slaves are simple-minded creatures that need to be told what's good for them," Craig continued coldly. "They'll bolt as soon as they get the chance. If Markus were any kind of businessman, he'd see that breeding the working slaves under controlled conditions is the only way to increase our numbers and ensure their loyalty."

Corin shook his head in horror. He got the distinct impression that controlled conditions did not involve allowing the slaves to choose who they wanted to breed with. "That's rape," he rasped in disgust. Granted, the act was nothing new to pleasure slaves, but the thought of Heather, *his sisters*, being impregnated by the kind of men who'd used him his entire life both sickened and enraged him.

"That's reality," Craig snarled, then readapted his tempered façade of diplomacy. "So I've decided to leave him with a parting message — that slaves will turn on their Masters no matter how accommodating they are. And that, my boy, is where you come in. Josh here has been kind enough to inform me that your Master treats you like a cherished possession, supporting your family and demanding nothing in return from them, just like he wants to do with all working slaves."

Corin looked to Josh to find the jealous truth written on his face. He'd known the man was petty and envious of his position, but to stoop to such an underhanded act as to put Corin's life in jeopardy for involuntarily usurping a role that was never his to begin with, was beyond despicable.

"So, I've come to offer you the privilege of being my slave. Taking you will teach Markus a lesson in the error of his ideals."

"You said you would take me, not him," Josh whined piteously. "You said you were just going to hurt him a little."

Craig swung to hit him again, but missed as Josh dropped to his knees in fear. The other slave didn't move in time to avoid the swift kick to his abdomen, however. "Oppose me again and I'll silence you permanently."

Corin stared aghast at the audacity of both men. How could Craig possibly think he'd jump at the chance to trade one monster for another? No. In his eyes, Markus was no longer the man he'd once attached that label to. His Master was generous and wanted him for reasons that didn't revolve around revenge or hate. Discovering the potentiality of Markus' plans for the slaves in his territory merely escalated his warming opinion of the man.

"No," he answered, with no little amount of incredulity in his voice.

Craig's face darkened with barely bridled fury. "I advise you to rethink your decision. I want you to come willingly, and you don't want to know the hell I'll put you through if you refuse."

Corin's breath caught in his throat with renewed fear at the sadistic gleam in Craig's narrowed eyes, yet he couldn't give in. Though Markus had turned Corin's life upside down with his absolute domination, he'd also treated him with more kindness than any man ever had. His soft touches and passion-filled kisses were things Corin was loath to give up for the possession of any other Master. He was a slave without freedom, but he was Markus' slave, and had no inclination to become another's.

"I will not go with you, willingly or otherwise," he said, the force of his conviction hiding the tremors racking his body.

Craig curled his lip. "That's a shame. I would've liked to have had something as pretty as you at my feet." He took off his jacket and holster, handed them to one of his men then slid his belt from the loops of his pants. "Guess I'll just have to make a different example out of you, then."

When the man started forward with the strap of leather wrapped around his fist, Corin searched frantically for something to defend himself with and grabbed the only thing within reach. He snatched up the alarm clock and threw it, spinning for the bathroom as he heard an angered curse in response. Craig yanked him back by his hair and threw him to the floor. There was no time to think, or even breathe, as a volley of booted feet bashed into him from all sides. Corin could do no more than try to curl in on himself as Craig and his men viciously attacked every part of his unprotected body.

Pain blazed and consumed his mind as they delivered punishing kicks for what seemed like several interminable minutes. When a few well-placed boots landed particularly savage blows to his ribs, piercing stabs shot through his chest, as if his bones had cracked under the brutal force. Just when he thought he might pass out from the inability to suck in air, the men relented and Craig's hard voice breached the roar in his ears.

"Strip him down and hold him on the bed."

Corin struggled weakly as his clothes were ripped away and he was thrown onto the bed. A man at each corner held down his limbs in bruising grips that stretched him fully across the mattress.

"Damn, look at all the marks on his back," Craig said excitedly. "This one must be a pain slut." He buried a hand in Corin's hair and wrenched his head up. "Do you like pain, bitch?" Without waiting for an answer, he added, "Then you're going to love what I'm about to do to you, but trust me, I'm going to get a lot more pleasure out of this than you will."

Corin couldn't stop the whimper that slipped out as Craig released his hair then stepped out of his vision. At the first blazing lash of the belt on his already abused flesh, Corin let out a sharp cry. The leather came down in a flurry of brutal strikes that flooded him with agony. Craig was meticulous in his assault, striking every inch of Corin's exposed skin, even hitting his arms and calves, but paying special attention to his ass. Corin screamed until his voice gave out and he was reduced to coughing sobs that jolted his battered ribs. He drowned in the relentless misery raining down upon him—the pain so great it stole his ability to retreat into his mind as he'd so often done in the past to escape his torment.

When the blows finally ended, he heard Craig order his men to turn him over onto his back. He moaned raggedly at the feel of the coarse comforter on his ravaged skin, helpless to flinch away when Craig leaned in close to peer down maliciously.

"Don't worry. The good part's coming soon, but I want to make sure you don't enjoy it as much as I will."

Corin watched helplessly as the belt was brought down again, this time across his fear-shriveled cock and balls. Renewed screams were torn from his raw throat as a blinding torrent of fire seared through him.

Over and over again, the belt struck the most sensitive parts of his body and his mind grayed, teasing him with the gift of unconsciousness, but holding it at the edge his grasp. Toward the end, Corin was near delirious and silently begging for it to stop, unable to give voice to the words. Tears streamed down the sides of his face as he stared at the blurred ceiling above.

A surreal haze began to cloud his mind, allowing him the retreat he'd been seeking, though he found it was at a cost he didn't want to pay.

His thoughts seemed to move beyond the agony to the panic of what might come next. What if this wasn't enough for Craig? What if he chose to kill him, rather than be satisfied with torturing his enemy's pet? Madeline and Amy would only have each other to depend on, and maybe Heather, if Markus didn't send them away. Somehow, Corin didn't think his Master would do that, but he couldn't put that much faith in the leader's frame of mind after this. Markus was already so detached from certain aspects of the world around him. Only Amy had been able to encourage a genuine smile past his stern personality, that Corin knew of.

Corin shuddered to think of what the man would do if he found his coveted possession beaten and murdered, despite his efforts to keep him safe. Would he unwittingly fall for Craig's twisted lesson and give up on his plans to free working slaves?

When the torment finally came to a halt and hands flipped him back over, roughly pulling him toward the foot of the bed, he knew he would fight until his last breath. He owed that much to his Master and to the future of his sisters. His dangling legs were kicked apart and he used the last of his strength to try to scramble away from the blunt tip of Craig's cock pressing harshly against his exposed hole.

When the man yelled loudly, he expected to feel the blinding pain of forced entry but was released instead. Sounds of furious shouts and gunfire rang in his ears, interspersed with booming crashes, as though the furniture was being flung at the walls. His body slumped listlessly to the floor and he shifted his face toward the scene in the middle of the room, heart leaping in sudden relief.

Markus' personal guards, as well as two others, attacked Craig's men with calculated wrath while his Master's massive form stood out in the center of the fray, both beautiful and terrifying at the same time. He wielded his knife with uncanny precision, deflecting Craig's own and slicing through flesh as though carving a work of art. The other man never stood a chance. With a final stab to the sternum, Markus ended his life, shoving the limp body off the length of his blade with the sole of his boot.

The fight was over in a matter of seconds and before Corin could blink, Markus was leaning over him. Corin gazed up in amazement at the fear lurking behind the rage in his Master's dark eyes, the moment shattering abruptly when his aching body was lifted and all he could focus on was forcing shallow breaths in and out of his bruised lungs.

"Get the doctor. Now!" Markus shouted.

The vibrations of his deep voice pounded through Corin's head, making him cringe from the volume, even though his ears still rang from the reverberations of the gunshots. He wanted to tell his Master to be quiet, to put him down, to take away the pain, but his overloaded brain did the job for him. Without warning, his eyes rolled back and his mind slipped over the edge and into darkness.

Chapter Thirteen

Corin's gradual entry into awareness was hampered by an invisible net that seemed reluctant to let him go. With a sense of urgency that beat at his emerging consciousness, he pushed at it relentlessly, trying to break through its heavy barrier. Something had happened. An issue of great import that played on the cliff of his thoughts, hanging just out of reach.

As his mind grappled to remember, a low hum of voices in the background grew to distinction. He recognized his Master's tone first, slightly off kilter and lacking its normally reserved confidence. It sounded as if he were having a heated argument with several others and when Corin blinked open his eyes, he saw all of them gathered near the foot of the bed he was lying in.

"I'm well aware of the situation," Markus was saying, his customary five o'clock shadow grown out to a shaggy stubble and his short, brown hair ruffled and spiked in some places. Corin could barely make out the dark creases of lines around his eyes and forehead that hadn't been there before, as he paced the width of the room.

"I don't think you do," another man with the regal looks of a diplomat said. "This will plunge us into a war we're unprepared for."

"We're already at war," Markus growled.

"Markus is right," a third man said. Corin recognized him as one of his Master's personal guard. Parland, if he recalled correctly — a bear of a man only a few inches shorter than his leader. "We can't say for sure this was done simply to force our hand in an ongoing issue."

"Then what else could it be?" the diplomat asked. "He obviously meant to get caught, else he would've taken what he came for and left."

"Are you sure none of your files were tampered with?" a second guard queried.

Markus shook his head. "None. I don't think he was after those, and I don't think he planned on us finding him. If the man I'd posted outside of my room hadn't stayed alive long enough to broadcast snatches of Craig's voice on his radio, I'd have never known what was going on. He had to have another motive."

"I spoke to Thomas about a half hour ago," Parland informed. "He hasn't made any progress on Josh yet. I'm starting to think that boy will hold his tongue no matter how much he's beaten."

The dignitary pinched his pointed chin in contemplation. "Perhaps Tulaine means to steal our slaves out from beneath us. Craig had already bought Josh. Maybe he tried to carry out his father's plan by starting with your slave."

Markus paused in his stride to peer out of the window into the black night beyond. "Possibly. Whatever the case, Tulaine will want to wage a full-scale war once he finds out about his son's death. My plans will have to be put on hold indefinitely, if not permanently."

Corin shook his head, small tendrils of alarm winding their way through his chest. Their assumptions were wrong, and Markus was falling prey to the very lesson Craig had set out to deliver in the first place. Even in death, the man was insinuating his dark seed of doubt. "No," Corin mouthed, but nothing came out of his sore, parched throat. After swallowing repeatedly, he tried again and managed a grating croak. Markus' head whipped around, his sharp eyes narrowing in on his slave.

"Leave us," the leader commanded. The men obeyed instantly and filed silently out of the room while Markus skirted the bed to sit on the side. From the nightstand, he picked up a bottle standing next to a glass of water and shook out two pills then brought them to Corin's lips.

"No," Corin said again in a hoarse whisper, turning his head from the drugs. He remembered everything now, and though his entire being thrummed with a bone-deep ache, he wanted to be sober for the coming conversation.

"Take the pills," Markus ordered in the imperious tone Corin was so familiar with.

"I have to tell you—"

"I will not repeat myself, boy. You may be allowed to speak only after you take them."

Corin glared openly at the man, weighing the pros and cons of his defiance. On the one hand, what he had to say was more important than the intimidation he felt under his Master's hard stare. And on the other, Markus could very well choose to punish him by calling the doctor to administer a more powerful drug that would knock him out completely. His Master had done it before when he'd had him branded.

Reluctantly, Corin opened his mouth and accepted the pills.

When Markus lifted him with one arm behind his neck, he almost spit the vile-tasting medicine out as shards of pain lanced through his sides. The bones of his ribcage felt as if they might break out of his skin and he wrapped his arms around them in a desperate attempt to hold them together. Markus touched the rim of the glass to his lips, but Corin couldn't concentrate enough to open up again until he heard the strong command from his Master. Once the pills were down and his body was laid flat, he took a moment to regain his composure.

"Turn over."

Corin cracked his lids to see the blue jar containing the cream used on his bruises in Markus' hand. He shook his head adamantly this time, knowing he wouldn't be able to think straight while it was being applied. "I want to talk first."

"You can talk while I'm putting this on," Markus said, twisting off the top.

"No. Before."

"Boy, you will obey me."

"No, *you* need to listen to *me!*" Corin rasped as loudly as he could, as shocked by his vehement rebellion as it appeared that his Master was. While he didn't think he could get through a physical punishment in his current condition if the man chose to deliver one, he also didn't believe he'd have to. His suspicion was confirmed when Markus stiffened and sat back, placing the jar on the nightstand.

Taking as deep a breath as he could, Corin started with a question—the one that had urged him into wakefulness and presided over his thoughts since his talk with Craig. "Do you really plan on freeing the working slaves?"

Markus sat forward with narrowed eyes, his interest piqued. "Who told you that?"

"Craig did," he whispered with an involuntary shudder.

Scrubbing his face roughly, Markus sighed and looked away. "I did want to but... I don't see how that can happen now. Tulaine will throw everything he has at us and I'll need every eligible man in the territory to defend it. Even if I promised the slaves their independence if they fought for me, many of them wouldn't. It would take some time for them to build up their confidence and loyalty after so many years, in some cases lifetimes, of those qualities being beaten out of them. The only way they would fight is if they were commanded to."

"Because you killed Craig."

Markus' ruggedly handsome features took on a frightening fierceness and he growled, "I would kill anyone who tried to hurt you."

Oh, God. He'd guessed at it, after learning of his Master's past and seeing his actions regarding Madeline and Amy. He'd even fancied it the truth after listening to Craig's claims, but to hear it from Markus' own lips made him shiver in awe. His Master truly did desire him as more than a body to use. He *needed* him, just as he'd needed his family. And like his family, he would willingly protect his slave, no matter the cost. Corin had seen the irrefutable proof with his own eyes when he'd been sprawled on the floor, watching his Master commit an act that would plunge their territory into an all-out war.

He was wanted by a man beyond all reason, and instead of terrifying him, the knowledge sent blossoming coils of warmth spiraling through his blood. His mouth curved in a slow smile that dispelled most of the confusion he'd been suffering since being traded into Markus' possession. He still didn't know why the man had chosen him, or even how he felt about being cherished by the leader, but it definitely wasn't unpleasant.

Markus frowned and tilted his head. "You find that amusing?"

"Yes. No. I just..." Damn, he'd had a point to make somewhere in all of this. Which was..."You can't," he blurted out as his train of thought came rushing back.

"I can't kill someone who means to do you harm?"

"You can't give up on freeing the slaves. That's exactly what Craig wanted, don't you see? You have his father by the balls and he got scared when you refused to agree to his terms. When Josh told him how much you..." he faltered at the choice of words Craig had used to describe him. Would Markus become angry and shun him for daring to think that he was more than a lowly pleasure slave to his Master? *And why should I care?* he silently berated himself. Yet he did, and he couldn't deny that it would hurt if he were castigated by the man whose every action had made him feel important.

"How much you c-covet me, he wanted to use me against you. He thought that if I left with him, willing to become his slave, you would see how traitorous all slaves are and give up on your plans to free them."

After a long, tension-filled pause, Markus said, "He did this — hurt you — because you refused."

It wasn't a question, but Corin nodded in affirmation anyway. The molten heat that blazed in his Master's eyes was fascinating to see, and gone in the next heartbeat. Markus stood abruptly and let out a roar that echoed along the walls, followed by a string of curses that made Corin glad they were aimed at a dead man and not him. The rant went on for several minutes, during which he didn't move, didn't speak. While the fear that bloomed in his chest was not born of the possibility that his Master might turn his fit of rage on him, it was still a paralyzing thing to watch.

Markus stopped suddenly, visibly willed the storm to pass through his large frame then walked back to the bed. "I swear to you this won't happen again."

Corin merely nodded, confident in the man's promise.

"I have a friend in the mid-western territory that I would trust with my life—and with yours. As soon as you're able to travel, I'll send you down there with Heather and your sisters, as well as a group of my men. They'll stay with you until I'm positive any threats to you have passed. I'll, uh..." Markus swallowed heavily and clenched his fists. "I'll make sure all of you have everything you could want."

That, he hadn't expected. Corin stared, wide-eyed and dumbfounded, as the implications of his Master's decree seeped into his disbelieving mind. "I could run," he whispered. Markus' eyes seemed to dull with... Was that sorrow?

"You won't need to. My men will only be there to keep you safe. I'm setting you free. This compound and the other will be the first places Tulaine will hit when he launches his attack. I can't risk your life by keeping you here and if you succeed in escaping again while I'm at war, I won't be able to take the time to find you. This is the only option."

"I d-don't understand."

"You're free, Corin," Markus said in a stronger tone. "I give you my word as your leader, not your Master."

Corin stared and waited — for the other shoe to drop, for him to wake up, for the joy and relief he'd always thought he would feel if he were ever to have his independence restored—but none of that came. Instead, he experienced a renewed sense of confusion, apprehension, and a deep-seated ache that started in his temples and spread to his throat and heart. This was what he'd wanted his entire life, a chance to live without pain, submission and ever-present fear. Better than that, he was being given a golden ticket of financial support which would keep him off the streets.

It was his dream.

"No."

Markus creased his forehead. "No?"

It was Corin's turn to swallow as sweat beaded on his brow. What the hell was he doing? He hated this man, didn't he? Markus had broken his will, humiliated and punished him repeatedly. If he stayed, none of that would change, much less stop altogether. He knew Markus was the kind of man that would dominate his partner, even if slavery weren't in effect — had witnessed the man's arousal at his subjugation almost daily and been forced to take pleasure in the sensual wielding of his body.

Yet, Markus had proven to be the Master Heather had praised from the very beginning. It was because of him his sisters were safe and loved by a childless mother who'd taken them into her heart as she would have her own flesh and blood. And now that man was giving him a chance at a self-governing future if he chose to leave without asking for anything in return.

Corin told himself all of these things, still not quite able to admit the real reason why he was indulging in insanity and throwing away what was probably the only opportunity he would ever get to be free. So, he came up with the next best thing.

"I want to stay to help you free the slaves. I can assist you with budgeting resources and talking to slaves about your proposal." Though it was a long stretch as he was completely uneducated except for what he'd learned at the hotel, he truly did want to participate in the leader's plan any way that he could.

Markus moved faster than he could react. With one hand he threw the covers back, scooped up a dollop of cream then brought that hand down on Corin's exposed cock. Corin cried out at the cold shock and agony of the light touch, trying to curl his limbs and roll away, but Markus held him fast. Corin's only recourse was to grab onto the fingers surrounding his searing member in an attempt to tear them away without causing himself more damage. It felt like Markus' palm was embedded with razors that cut into his most sensitive area and he bit his tongue so hard that blood coated his mouth.

"Look at what was done to you," Markus demanded softly.

Hesitantly, he tilted his chin to peer down the stretch of his wrapped torso through tear-filled eyes. Only the head of his cock was showing, the sight enough to wrench a sob from his chest. It was dark purple, striped in blistering, red welts and crusted at the tip from dried blood and fluids that had leaked out. Corin looked back up at Markus, working his throat convulsively to reign in his horror.

"W-will it...?" *Oh, God, no, please, no.*

"Spencer says there was no permanent damage, but I couldn't prevent this from happening to you. Now tell me truthfully why you would risk going through this or worse to stay here," Markus demanded, moving his slack yet iron fist up and down Corin's shaft and spreading the cream over its flaccid length.

Corin didn't want to answer, the unhurried motion sending ripples of unbearable fire dancing along his skin and spearing through his gut. Tears spilled over his lashes at the onslaught, though whether they were due to pain or the anxiety of Markus' order, he wasn't sure. Unable to take any more, he sobbed, "I w-want to be needed."

Markus' hand stilled. After several excruciating seconds, he leaned forward and took Corin's mouth in a passionate kiss, driving past trembling lips and exerting his dominance with the powerful sweeps of his tongue. By the time his Master drew back, he had no more strength or desire to struggle against his authority.

"If you stay here, I will never let you go again. Even if I manage to free all of the slaves in my territory, you will still belong to me."

Corin shivered at the implacable tone and the knot of tension in his clenched stomach slowly unfurled. Meeting Markus' unwavering gaze with new-found determination, he whispered, "Yes, Master."

* * * *

"You look like you're doing much better."

Corin turned from the sink full of dishes to see Heather standing behind him. It had been two weeks since the incident with Craig and he could finally wear clothes without cringing at the least brush of fabric across his skin. While there was still some bruising and more scars to add to his collection, that didn't bother him overmuch. It was sleeping in the same bed where the incident had occurred which was the hard part. At least once a night he woke up screaming, drenched in a cold sweat. It had taken him a while to figure out why he was having nightmares now when he hadn't since he'd been a small child and just learning to fear. It was because in that bed, despite the trauma of being made a slave, he'd always felt safe, secure in his Master's strong embrace.

That feeling had been robbed by Craig and no matter how many times Markus soothed him throughout the night, he couldn't bring himself to look at the bed without recalling what had been done there. As much as he wanted to stay here, he had to admit he was glad to be leaving. His new bed wouldn't have his Master in it to hold him, but neither would it evoke memories better left with the dead.

Tulaine had yet to make a move and the delay in retaliation for the death of his son was making everyone nervous. Even the random skirmishes that'd been going on for some time had stopped. Markus had claimed he suspected the other leader of amassing his forces for a full-scale attack, in which case both compounds would likely be the main targets. He'd requisitioned an old military barracks that had been converted into a clothing factory to house all those ill-equipped to deal with the coming war. Heather, Corin, his sisters and Madeline's art instructor were among them. It was in a district roughly an hour away and Markus had arranged for them to leave on the morrow, informing Corin that he would visit every weekend.

Corin smiled at Heather. "I am."

One corner of her mouth lifted in a small quirk, her bright eyes sparkling ruefully. "And something tells me it's not only because you're nearly healed."

Warmth crept into his cheeks and he went back to scrubbing the dishes. "I don't hate him anymore, if that's what you mean."

"Nor certain parts of his anatomy?" she asked in a hushed voice. "I saw you looking at his crotch instead of the floor yesterday like a good little slave should." She clucked her tongue and Corin turned again to gape.

His Master had taken to using his mouth every day, giving his body time to recover, and finding other means to stimulate Corin's arousal. Without the smog of animosity on Corin's end, it was strangely erotic — and more than a little frustrating. Markus teased him unrelentingly every night, finding ways he'd never imagined could make his body come alive with pleasure, only to deny his orgasm each time. Corin was both yearning for release and scared of it at the same time. The sting of urination had ceased only a few days ago and bruises still marked the length of his cock. Would the aching pain return when it became fully engorged?

Grabbing the spray nozzle next to the faucet, he aimed it at Heather and shot a stream of water at her. She sputtered with eyes wide in shock. Gales of laughter burst from Madeline and Amy, who were sitting at the table playing dominos.

"I can't believe you just did that!" Heather gasped, then leaped to the sink and flicked a splash of dish water at him. They laughed, soaking each other through in their water duel until Madeline raised her voice above theirs.

"I think it's time for us to get going. Amy and I still need to pack."

"Yay! I wanna to use the Tinker Bell suitcase Markus got for me," Amy said, jumping up from the table and bouncing on her feet.

"Tinker Bell?" Corin looked to Heather, who rolled her eyes.

"I never figured Master for a family guy, but he spoils the hell out of these brats," she said with an affectionate grin. "Took me hours to get Amy to bed after her sugar high from all the candy he had one of his men get the other day."

Corin shook his head. He didn't think he would ever figure his Master out. The man was gruff, stern and especially aloof around the girls, as if he didn't know how to respond to them, yet he constantly showered them with gifts.

Heather clapped her hands, saying, "All right, let's clean up then we'll go."

As they straightened the area, Corin finished the dishes then saw them to the door. He asked Heather to wait with Amy while he pulled Madeline to the side. There'd been no time of late to sit down and talk privately, and her subdued manner was starting to worry him.

"How are you holding up?"

Eyes of dark honey met his with a hesitant expression. "I'm okay. It's just a little weird, you know?"

"Yeah, I do." He tucked a wavy lock of hair behind one of her ears. "Are you happy, though?"

Madeline nodded and smiled faintly. "Heather's great, and so is Markus. I just..." Her delicate brows drew down as her throat worked convulsively. "I don't understand how Mom could protect me from

Dad then sit by while her new husband hit me. And Dad..." She let out an exasperated, disgusted huff, then asked quietly, "Cory, I knew he beat you, but did he ever...? Did he sell you to some of the guests staying at the hotel?"

Corin's heart constricted in a rush of shame that flooded his system. As smart as she was, it was foolish to think she hadn't realized what was going on those nights when Scott or Doreen would cover for him at the front desk while he earned back their lost profits. Still, he couldn't bring himself to voice the truth. She'd loved Scott, for what he was worth, and retained a measure of innocence Corin didn't want to destroy.

"Addie, what he tried to do to you was wrong." He attempted to pull her into his arms but she lifted a hand to stop him.

"I need an answer. Please, tell me," she pleaded.

He sighed and lowered his hands. "Yeah, he did."

Tears shimmered in Madeline's eyes before she blinked them away and firmed her shoulders. "Thank you. I can hate him now. I thought maybe it was me, but now I know it was all him."

This time when he pulled her into a hug, she didn't resist. "It was never you, Addie. *Never you.* I'm sorry I couldn't get you out of there in time."

She wrapped her arms around his midsection and squeezed, nodding her head. "I love you, Cory."

"Love you, too," he said, placing a kiss on her temple. When they broke apart, he wiped the fallen tears from her cheeks and kissed her again. "I'll see you in the morning."

She gave him a watery but true smile, then left. Corin went around to the other side of the penthouse and glared malevolently at the huge bed. Images flashed through his mind and his cock twitched responsively, once again preventing him from following his Master's orders to kneel by the recliner and wait until they could go to sleep together. Corin knew Markus was trying to ease his discomfort by not demanding he wait for him in the bed, yet just having the thing in sight was enough to set his nerves on edge.

The punishment delivered every night for his disobedience, he could deal with. They were never done cruelly and, in fact, always left him craving his Master's touch even more. The memories with no one there to comfort him, he could not.

His thoughts spanned back to the week before, when Josh's fate had been decided regarding his involvement in Craig's plan. Upon Corin's request, his Master had allowed him to visit the other slave in one of the cells of the jail in the other compound before the final ruling had been made. For all that it would've been justified, Corin hadn't been able to dredge up the animosity he'd once felt for the man, not when he'd seen the real pain burning in the depths of Josh's haunted gaze.

During his talk with the other man, he'd discovered that Josh had been born into the life of a pleasure slave, trained then later bought and sold more times than he could remember. Markus had been the first Master to treat him with kindness and decency, and what he'd perceived as the loss of that through his elevation to a work slave and Corin's presence had, in his eyes, stolen his chance to find love.

Through bitter and spiteful anger, Josh had admitted that he was in love with the leader. Corin had secretly thought the man's misplaced emotions stretched beyond the limitations of simple, unrequited love. Josh was one of the few slaves he'd met that truly desired to serve and relinquish his body and rights to a Master who would value him. After being cared for with the passion Markus had shown him, Corin couldn't honestly say he now desired anything less. A slave learned to accept what it was given, but what happened when human cravings for more came into play?

As skewed and malicious as Josh's attempts had been to strike out at the man who'd given him up for another, Corin hadn't been able to find it in his heart to hate him. Josh craved love that'd never been given to him, and his venture to find it had caused more damage than anyone could inflict on him at this point. Out of pity, Corin had convinced Markus to lessen Josh's sentence to one of servitude in a factory bordering the outskirts of the territory. There would remain a slave for the rest of his years, but that wasn't to say the future couldn't change. Heather had found compassion in the darkest hours of her life at a similar factory and, perhaps, so could Josh.

Turning on his heel, Corin went to the laundry basket, took off his wet clothes and tossed them in.

His Master's binder sitting on the end table next to the recliner caught his eye. Curiosity got the better of him and he walked around to pick it up. Inside were categorized folios from businesses all around the territory. Corin rifled through the papers, seeing nothing that made a lot of sense to him until he got to the last page. Behind it was a clear sheet protector holding the picture Amy had drawn for Markus almost three weeks ago. It showed Corin, his sisters and what could only be Markus in his towering form, all holding hands and smiling. There was a wrinkled crease in the center as if the paper had been folded and unfolded several times.

How often had Markus looked at it before putting it in the binder?

Corin's throat tightened as he ran his fingertips over the drawing, recalling the smile on his Master's face when Amy had given it to him. There were miracles in the world, and his sister was definitely one of them.

Chapter Fourteen

After replacing the binder, he knelt in front of the door and waited patiently. An hour later, his Master came in and paused in the doorway.

"Stubborn boy," Markus muttered in a tone that lacked malice. They both knew Corin wasn't being intentionally obstinate. From his pocket, he withdrew a small carabiner and linked the loops on Corin's cuffs together in front. "Come."

He followed his Master to the bed and watched him take off his weapons in lazy movements. When Markus sat down on the side of the mattress and patted his leg, Corin knew what was expected of him. Lying across his Master's thighs with his ass in the air, he braced his hands on the floor for purchase and tensed in anticipation. The spanking would be swift and harsh, but well worth it. One hand pressed in between his shoulder blades while another smoothed over his buttocks in preparation.

The first strike knocked a grunt from him and he bit into his bottom lip to stifle a cry. His Master's cupped palm fell on him again, pushing him forward and sending streaks of fire across his skin and into his muscles. In rapid succession the brutal slaps came, and even though there were only ten in all, he was winded and close to begging by the end of it. Markus ran a hand over his behind in a soothing motion to relieve the burning sting that enflamed it. For a moment, the hand was gone and when it came back, a saliva-slicked finger ran down the cleft of his ass. It circled the tight ring there then slowly pushed in.

Corin moaned and felt his cock begin to swell against the rough material of Markus' jeans at the piercing intrusion. It wasn't exactly pleasure-inducing yet, but his body responded to his Master's touch like it'd been trained to do. Another finger was added and his breaths quickened further as they forked in and out, testing the resilience of his quivering entrance. Then they speared in and curved, hitting that spot that lit him like a spark. Blood defied gravity and pooled in his groin, filling his aching member and enticing small whimpers from his lips. When his hips began to swivel of their own accord, Markus swatted his ass smartly with his other hand. A warning, but that was all he needed. If he continued to move without permission, his Master would torture him like this for as long as he felt it necessary for Corin to learn his lesson, no matter how tired he was.

"Have you packed all of your things?" Markus asked.

"Y-yes, Master."

"Good. When I come down on the weekend, this is mine until I leave. You will not step out of the bedroom unless I'm with you, and I don't plan on going anywhere until I need to return to the compound." To emphasize his point, he pushed in a third finger and rubbed mercilessly on that spot.

Corin jerked and moaned again. "Yes, M-Master," he whispered, his cock throbbing at the pressure in his channel. Markus kept him there for several minutes, driving Corin insane with the need to move and holding him on the edge of climax.

The merciless massage came to an abrupt end, however, when a blast of static erupted from the intercom, interspersed with tinny, popping noises and shouted words.

"Sir, we're under attack!" a man yelled. "They're coming in through the Market and left wing. I've already dispatched some of the men, but we need you down in the front."

Corin scooted away as Markus cursed and jumped up to speak through the intercom. "I'm on my way." Bending down to unfasten Corin's cuffs, he ordered, "Get dressed. We're leaving."

With a surge of adrenaline racing through him, he scrambled over to the suitcase he'd packed earlier and withdrew a clean outfit to put on. "I can call Heather to bring my sisters up here. You should go to your men."

Markus turned a fierce glare on him while strapping on his weapons. "My men can hold their own until I get you to safety. This room is unsecure and I'll not take a chance with your life. Hurry, boy."

Corin didn't say anything else. As soon as he was finished getting ready, Markus ushered him from the penthouse with a firm hand on his wrist, making him run to keep up. They took the stairs across from the elevator to the eighth floor, where Markus pounded on Heather's door. She answered immediately in a white robe, hair damp and tangled from having been recently washed.

"Get the girls," Markus said. "We're at war."

That was all it took. Heather sprang into action and ran to the room adjoined to hers. With Markus' permission, Corin followed her and helped to rush his sisters into changing their pajamas for street clothes.

"What's going on?" Madeline asked, eyes wide with the panic she was obviously picking up on.

"We've got some trouble and need to hide, sweetie," Heather answered in a surprisingly calm voice. "Don't be afraid. Master will take care of this and come get us when it's over."

The conviction in her tone eased some of Corin's anxiety. He knew his Master was a skilled fighter and the fact that he was taking the time to see them to a safe spot in the midst of an emergency filled him with faith in the man's ability to protect them.

Markus led them back to the stairs and down to ground level. Before exiting, he palmed his gun and checked the corridor then, finding it clear, ushered them out. Toward the end leading to the commons area, three men emerged from one of the doors. Markus raised his gun and fired without hesitation, hitting each one in the head before they had a chance to aim their own firearms. It was a mark of his dedication as a leader that he knew instantly friend from foe. To Corin, they appeared no different than his Master's soldiers.

When Amy screamed, he gathered her up and motioned for Heather and Madeline to precede him. They ran through several hallways, pausing only for Markus to check each path before taking off again. Finally, they emerged from an exit and spilled out into the brisk, night air. Distant gunshots and loud explosions could be heard over the shouts of soldiers running in all directions. A ball of fire lit the dark sky to their left and the stench of sulfur and smoke clogged Corin's nostrils.

"Follow me," Markus yelled over the cacophony.

As they raced after him, Corin recognized the exit as the same one they'd brought his sisters through on the night they'd arrived at the compound. There were four buildings opposite them of various sizes that formed a half-circle. Markus led them to the smallest one on the far right. It was a single story and contained several desks with computers lined against three of the four walls. In one corner, Markus kicked over a rug on the hardwood floor to reveal a trapdoor beneath. He grabbed onto the collapsible ring and yanked hard, the hinges creaking loudly from disuse.

The steep wooden staircase descending into the interior of the room below was swallowed up by utter darkness. Markus grabbed a flashlight from the top stair, clicked it on and handed it to Corin. "Do you know how to use a gun?"

Corin nodded. He'd never handled one before, but had seen Scott clean and load his several times.

"Good. There's a cache in a chest down there. The pistols should already be loaded. No matter what happens, do not leave that room until I come for you."

"Master—"

"Get in there now!" Markus barked, pointing toward the stairs.

Heather and Madeline flew down the steps and Corin carried Amy in after them. The door was closed as soon as they were all in and heavy shadows fell around them. The relative silence in the wake of the chaos above was near deafening. Corin handed Amy off to Heather then used the flashlight to survey their surroundings. They were in a small basement with cement walls and sparse furniture layered in years of dust. He strode over to two large chests lying against the back wall and opened the first to reveal a myriad of firearms and what appeared to be an assortment of bombs and grenades. He checked the safety on one of the pistols on top then searched the other chest. That one held blankets, medical supplies, ropes, portable radios and more flashlights.

He stood a second flashlight up on the ground to provide them with additional light then took out two blankets, shook them free of dust and gave them to Heather and Madeline There was no warmth in the room and no way of knowing how long they would be holed up in it.

"I'm scared," Amy whispered from Heather's lap, who'd taken a seat on one of the chests.

"I know, baby," Heather crooned. "It'll be all right. Master won't let anything happen to us. We just have to wait here until it's over."

"Who's fighting us?" Madeline asked, her teeth chattering slightly.

"The leader of the mid-southern territory. He's a bad man, but Master's been preparing for this. All of his men have, so there's no need to worry."

Madeline nodded weakly, looking about as convinced as Corin felt. He couldn't squelch the sense of impending danger, but his concern wasn't only for them. It was for Markus. Foolish, considering he'd seen the man in action and knew he could hold his own, yet the cold knot of dread in his gut wouldn't relent. He ventured over to the staircase and took a seat halfway up, straining his ears to listen for clues as to what was going on outside. They waited in silence as time stretched on, each lost in their own thoughts and fears.

After a while, Madeline stood and joined him on the stairs a few steps below him. "Do you love him?"

Corin looked down in consternation, too distracted to concentrate on her question. "What?"

"Your Master," she clarified. "Do you love him?"

Corin shook his head, wondering what the hell had prompted her to ask that at such an inopportune time. "I'm worried about him. That's all."

"And?"

Biting back a groan, he rifled a hand through his hair agitatedly. He'd forgotten how tenacious she could be while in the pursuit of answers. "He's my Master. A slave can't love who owns him."

She furrowed her pale brow and pulled the blanket tighter around her body. "Why not? I've seen the way he looks at you at times. Like you're the only person in the world. Like he loves you."

Corin froze, not quite comprehending the meaning of her words. He had known what he'd committed himself to when he'd chosen slavery over freedom. A life without the kind of love he'd always dreamt of. At the time, it hadn't exactly been a hardship. In fact, he hadn't felt like he was losing anything at all. There had only been the fear of never finding another who would give so much and ask for so little in return, and he could no longer claim that the use of his body was a violation. He desired his Master's dominating touch as much as Markus needed him.

"She's right, you know," Heather piped up. "In all the years I've known him, I've never seen him look at anyone the way he looks at you."

Corin deliberated on their words for all of two seconds. "Stay here. I'll be back as soon as I can."

"Where are you going?"

He jumped up, tucked the gun into the back of his pants and ascended the stairs. "I need to make sure he's okay. I won't be long. Heather, can you use one of the guns in the crate?" When she gave a hesitant nod, he shouldered open the trapdoor using all of his strength and peered outside to make sure the above room was clear.

"Cory!" Madeline called. When he turned in her direction, she smiled and said, "Be careful."

With a nod, he climbed out and quietly lowered the heavy door. At the entrance to the building were two soldiers with guns drawn, firing them occasionally at distant targets. Corin cursed. He should've known Markus wouldn't leave them without a guard. A glance around showed a window on the farthest wall and he hoisted himself onto the desk in front of it and pried open the latch. When the frame squealed in protest, he winced and shot a look at the guards, suppressing a sigh of relief to see them still focused on the enemy outside. Swiftly, he jumped out and stood against the wall, pulling the gun from his pants and taking off the safety.

His thoughts raced in an attempt to determine where his Master might be. The man over the intercom had said the enemy was coming in from the market and for Markus to meet them at the front. He had to have meant a location near the entrance to the market. It was the only building that gave access to both compounds, but Corin had no idea where he was in relation to that area. Skirting the compound they'd come from would involve too much exposure. Deciding to take his chances in the maze of hallways inside, he ran across the open distance separating the buildings and into the exit he'd come through earlier.

It was a laborious process of trial and error with the doors lining the hallways. There was no identifiable pattern to the ones leading to destinations other than rooms, requiring him to rely on chance and memory to find his way. Fortunately, he met no others and eventually came to the back exit of the laundry room. Sure of his path now, he sprinted to the kitchen and, after finding it empty, peaked through the door of the commons are. It, also, appeared to be vacated, though he still felt like a running bull's eye as he dashed across the long expanse and into the main corridor on the other side.

He was halfway down when two men barreled backwards through the far door, set upon by two others that crashed in after them. They fought viciously in hand-to-hand combat, too preoccupied to notice him, but he didn't want to stick around to see which of them came out victorious. Frantically checking the doors near him, he found one that was unlocked and slipped into the room. He scrubbed the sweat from his hands onto his jeans and listened with bated breath for the sounds of combat to fade. When there was silence once more, he peered out and, finding the way clear again, continued his flight.

The other side of the door was unmanned and the reverberation of gunfire blasted in rapid staccato was enough to make him cringe against the wall inside. The large area was completely devoid of the vendor stalls and tables it usually held, leaving the men within to find shelter behind the massive columns. Veiled in shadows with only half of the lights overhead having survived, it was impossible for Corin to make out facial features or even the colors of the soldiers' clothes.

He began to make his way in choppy sprints, using the columns to hide behind, toward the other compound. At only a quarter of the way, however, he caught a glimpse of a large figure that stood taller than the others from the corner of his eye. The man's movements were steady and deliberate, exceedingly calm under the circumstances in a way that was all too familiar to Corin. His heart pounded in his chest as the man stepped from behind a column to shoot and he recognized the silhouette of his Master.

In the next instant, everything changed.

Markus stumbled back as if he'd been punched and fell in an awkward heap to the floor, followed immediately by a pause in the barrage of gunfire aimed at him.

"Master!" The shout was wrenched from Corin's throat before he could consider the repercussions. With no crowds of people or wares to buffet his volume, his voice carried across the open space, gathering the attention of all those nearest him. With his horrified gaze locked onto Markus' unmoving form, he didn't see the gun that was pointed at his head, but he did hear the commands that were delivered in an imperious tone.

"Wait! That has to be the slave I heard about. Finish Markus off. I want to take care of this one myself."

A volley of cover fire rang out as Corin looked over to see the owner of the voice burst forth in his direction. Another man took off at a dead run toward Markus and it took all that Corin had not to try to outrun him. There was no way he would make it in time. Instead, he brought up his gun and fired several bullets, none of them hitting their mark. He was about to change his mind and run to Markus regardless, when the solid weight of the man aiming for him crashed into his side, knocking the gun from his hand. Shards of searing light exploded behind his eyes as his skull cracked sharply against the hard granite floor and the breath was knocked from his lungs. A fist came down on his fractured ribs and they shifted with grating pain under the punishing blow.

"You're the one responsible for my son's death, aren't you?"

When his vision finally cleared, he looked up into the features of a man that resembled Craig in every way except for the grizzled hair and flapping of his jowls as he spoke.

"I'm going to make you pay for what you did to him. Your Master ain't here to protect you now."

Anger surged through Corin, eating away at his fear as his mind registered the identity of the man on top of him. It was Tulaine—it had to be—blaming him for the sadistic faults of his son. When the man's fist reared back again, Corin slammed his knee into Tulaine's groin and wriggled out from beneath the significant bulk holding him down. Just as his fingertips grazed the handle of the gun that had skittered a few yards away, he was flipped over and straddled about the waist. The air was cut off from his lungs as Tulaine's hands ringed his neck and choked him mercilessly.

Rage blazed within the man's black eyes and he pressed down on the vulnerable windpipe in his grip. Corin stubbornly refused to give in to the paralysis of panic. He was tired of meekly accepting his fate, allowing others to place the responsibility of their careless actions onto him. If he was going to die, he would go out fighting for his right to live.

Forcing his grasping hands from those that held his throat, he searched blindly along Tulaine's hips until he felt the cold handle of a knife in its holster. Dark spots danced around the edges of his vision by the time he was able to yank it free and angled his wrist, plunging it with all of his waning strength into the fatty tissue of the man's side. Tulaine's body jerked and his eyes widened, but Corin didn't stop there. He pulled the blade out and stabbed again, and again. The haze of his bloodlust didn't recede until red, viscous ribbons poured from the man's mouth and splattered his cheek and forehead.

Only then did he see the blank slate of death remove all signs of life from the gaze which stared down at him. Tulaine slumped forward, crushing Corin with so much dead weight his lungs didn't have time to recuperate their loss of oxygen. He lay in an obscene embrace with the victim who would have been his murderer for what seemed an eternity, shaking violently with the pounding of bruised ribs that couldn't expand to take in precious air. His thoughts began to laze and he wondered how long it would take for death to claim him as well.

Then the body was suddenly snatched away. His autonomic nervous system punched into action in the next moment, his lungs trying to retain their function while his throat choked and coughed and his heart sped to pump blood throughout his weakened limbs.

"Corin. Fuck, *Corin!* Talk to me, damn it!"

Corin flinched as his shoulders were rattled, blinking open his eyes to see his Master's handsome face staring down at him. "I'm—" He coughed again jarringly at the scratch in his throat. "I'm f-fine." His whispered declaration didn't stop Markus from running his hands over the length of his body, however, questing for injuries and finally coming to a stop when only bruises were found.

But Markus was far from satisfied.

"What the hell were you thinking?" he growled, as he gently picked up Corin's limp form and cradled him to his chest. When Corin opened his mouth to reply, he snapped, "Don't answer that. We'll discuss this later."

"Sir," a man said from somewhere to the right. "Tulaine's dead."

Another man approached and held out his arms to try to take Corin from Markus. "I'll carry him back to your quarters."

"No," Markus barked. "I've got him. Spread the word to our enemy that they have a new leader now, but let them retreat and take their wounded. I'll deal with them later. Find Parland and have him meet me here as soon as he can. I'll be back shortly." He turned on his heel then, striding toward the entrance to the corridor without waiting for a response.

Corin didn't talk, didn't struggle or do anything other than allow the surrounding warmth of his Master to seep into his bones and chase away the image of Tulaine's hatred bearing down on him. It wasn't until they were outside and a cold night breeze wafted over them that he felt the chill of liquid soaked through the front of his shirt. He peered down, at first thinking the glistening sheen of blood that stained his shirt had come from Tulaine, then looked over to find Markus' front soaked through as well. Tracing with his fingers across the width of Markus' chest, he found a small hole and looked up when the man hissed.

"You were shot." He remembered now the shock of seeing his Master fall.

"It's nothing."

Corin shook his head. It wasn't "nothing". The bullet wound was leaking profusely. "You shouldn't be carrying me. You're hurt." He started to squirm, only to be stilled by the man's tightened grip.

"Behave or I will strip you down and punish you right here."

Corin growled in frustration, meeting his Master's half amused, half severe expression.

Markus sighed and the ghost of a grin lifted his lips. "I'll have Doc look at it."

"Sir?" One of the guards Markus had set to watch over the building Corin had been holed up in came running forward. "Is that...? Shit, I didn't see him get out. I swear—"

"Of course you didn't. My boy apparently has vanishing powers. He gets out again, though, and I'll see you stripped of rank, am I clear?"

"Yes, sir," both men responded simultaneously.

Markus continued to stare at the first then ordered abruptly, "Take off your shirt."

When the man hurried to comply, he set Corin on his feet and stripped him of his bloodied shirt, exchanging it for the clean one.

As the second soldier lifted the latch leading down to the basement, Markus raised Corin's chin so that their eyes met.

"I need you," he said fiercely.

After a tense pause, a flood of emotions tugged at Corin's heart and he recognized the sentence for the confession it was.

"Promise me you'll stay here until I come for you."

"I promise, Master."

Markus stared at him for several more seconds as though gauging the truth of his words, finally nodding once and urging him down the stairs. When the door above was closed, a chorus of gasps filled the sudden silence and Madeline rushed to him, performing the same inspection of his body that Markus had made earlier.

"What happened? Were you hurt? Are you all right?" Madeline asked in a frenzied rush.

"I'm okay," Corin answered, taking her hands into both of his and pushing them down.

"Is that blood on your cheek?"

"It's not mine," he assured her. "I swear to you I'm fine." He gazed into her worried eyes until he saw the reluctant acceptance of his words and wrapped her in a tight hug. Over her shoulder, he looked to Amy, who sat wide-eyed then to Heather, and smiled. His friend frowned at first then returned his smile, as if she knew what he couldn't get past the lump in his throat.

He'd seen it. That look Madeline and Heather had spoken of. The one that assured him he hadn't lost a damn thing when he'd turned down his chance at freedom. He was a slave with no more rights than those which his Master granted him, but he was loved. And somehow, that made all of his sacrifices worth it.

Chapter Fifteen

Markus

The soft mist of dawn's light flowed in through the windows, greeting Markus subtly as he cracked open his lids. For the first time in weeks, no...months, he felt invigorated upon waking. Ready to meet the demands of the day, and it was all due to the small wisp of a man resting peacefully along his lower abdomen. Markus feathered his fingers through his boy's silky, white-blond hair, fanning it out over his side. When he'd first seen Corin years ago, he'd been drawn instantly to the shade of defiance lurking just beneath his submissive nature. The wary, shuttered look in his almond-colored eyes that had shone with a strength of spirit he'd rarely seen in most men, let alone slaves.

Yet, he'd stifled the urge to make Corin his, knowing if he did, he wouldn't be able to let go. That level of commitment was something he hadn't been able to contemplate at the time. His heart had been shattered long ago with the deaths of everyone he'd loved, and with their lives had fled his capacity for humor, mercy and many of the morals his father had once instilled in him. Anger and hatred had been his constant companions with no room for the possibility of endangering his heart again by letting anyone else in, but when the opportunity to possess Corin had been made available, he hadn't been able to turn it down.

Little had he known that the man would have such a critical impact on his life. Corin's undying love for his sisters had reminded him, painfully at times, of the commitment he'd held for his own family. It had forced him to acknowledge the fact that he still wanted what had been so brutally taken from him. And when Corin had chosen him over freedom, it'd felt as if his heart might shatter all over again. That his boy, who'd been abused so harshly in his past, would willingly pass up an offer of freedom to remain his slave was near incomprehensible.

That Corin had gone against his orders and risked everything to check on him was entirely humbling. Because of him, Tulaine was dead, as well as the only one of his sons with an interest in ruling after him. The people of the mid-southern territory had already sent another delegation to conduct negotiations. However, Markus was in no hurry to start. The territory was his. All that need be discussed at this point were his plans for bringing new business to the areas and, consequently, freeing the slaves. Not all would be granted independence, such as most of the pleasure slaves like Corin, but it was a beginning.

Markus tensed as his boy began to stir, emitting small whimpers, as if caught in another one of his nightmares. He was aware that sleeping in the same bed where Craig had assaulted him was an issue, and in fact, Markus loathed sleeping in it for the same reason. The new bed he'd ordered to his specifications would be arriving, hopefully, within the next few days.

Pulling Corin up to his chest, he kissed his forehead lightly and whispered, "Wake up, boy. Come back to me."

Corin roused instantly like he always did, no doubt an ingrained response from years of having to live in fear, even in his sleep. "Master?"

"Shh, it's just me." Thickly fringed eyes peered up at him, innocently seductive, and Markus felt the embers of arousal bloom in his groin. He would never get enough of his boy, his tentative submission and innate need to be dominated. They were qualities Markus had recognized immediately and taken great pleasure in cultivating.

Cradling Corin's head in his hands, he guided him down, eager for the warmth of his boy's mouth encasing his semi-erect cock. Without hesitation, Corin flicked his tongue across the slit, swirled it around the head then brought his lips down to clasp tightly around the growing length. He used one hand to steady the base and the other to gently massage Markus' balls, rubbing a finger along his perineum and coaxing flames of desire to lick upon his skin. The suction his boy created, along with the friction of his tongue, soon had Markus rolling his hips with need.

Unable to hold back any longer, he removed Corin's hand from his cock, braced his skull and brought it down roughly. Sparks fired in his blood as the head of his full erection hit the back of Corin's throat. His boy's hands tightened around his balls and thigh in an attempt to hold on, but he was already too far gone to be patient. It had been over two weeks since he'd last buried himself deep in his slave's ass and knowing

Corin was healed and ready to accommodate his considerable girth was driving his arousal to an accelerated peak.

He brought Corin's mouth down over and over again, forcing him to take all that he had to give until the building pressure threatened to explode. With a grunt, he pulled his slave off and lightly slapped his cheek. "Turn around."

As Corin resituated himself so he straddled Markus' larger frame on hands and knees, his face hovering above Markus' groin and rigid erection bobbing downwards, Markus reached over and grabbed a bottle of lube from the drawer of the nightstand. He poured a good amount of liquid on his fingers and pressed them into the crease above him. Pushing two inside and reveling in the constriction of the ring around them and the gasp that came at the intrusion, he ordered, "Take my cock into your mouth, boy, and don't you dare use your hands. I want every last inch stretching your throat wide."

The moment Corin complied, he twisted his fingers and hooked them down, finding the fleshy nub of the prostate within and stroking it repeatedly. Corin moaned loudly and the vibrations it caused jolted his pulsing member. He added a third finger, forking them in and out while he used his other hand to cup the back of Corin's head, pushing his slave's lips to his pelvis and keeping them there. Muscles swallowed convulsively around the tip of his cock, working it with a talent he'd never experienced with anyone except his boy.

Judging Corin's hole relaxed enough to take him without tearing, he withdrew both hands and said, "Turn around again." He moved Corin to straddle his thighs and sat up to detach the link binding his cuffs then reattached it so that Corin's wrists were locked together behind his back. Lying back down, he dribbled lube onto his aching shaft and fisted it from root to tip, stimulated by his boy's rapt gaze and the quickening of his breaths.

"Come here." When Corin scooted up, raising himself onto his knees, Markus found his puckered entrance with the head of his cock then grabbed onto Corin's hips, keeping him poised in the vulnerable position. "You disobeyed me the other night by leaving the basement."

Corin looked at his chin with a slight frown, his breath coming in short pants. "Y-yes, Master."

Markus strengthened his grip and pulled down savagely, punching himself into his boy's resistant hole. Corin's pained cry, coupled with the scorching heat of his channel, drew a long groan from Markus' chest. His entire body strained with the effort to give Corin time to adjust. After several torturous seconds, he lifted his hands until only the head of his cock remained sheathed then slammed them down a second time.

"You will never disobey me again," he growled, punctuating each word with a brutal thrust of his hips.

"No, M-Master."

A more formal punishment would have to be conducted later, though there wasn't a doubt in his mind that his boy would likely disregard his lesson in the future if he felt he needed to. Yet somehow, that only made his heart swell with pride. Corin would never be the trustworthy slave to follow his Master's commands blindly. He was a protector, and because of that, the most valued thing in Markus' life. Still, that didn't hold him back from inflicting a little preliminary discipline.

Keeping one hand firmly on his boy's hip, he gripped his bobbing cock and began pumping it furiously. When Corin's head lolled back, his member weeping pre-cum under the aggressive handling, he pressed his thumb ruthlessly into the slit. Corin yelped and tried to squirm away, but Markus only picked up his relentless pace, driving himself harder and deeper into his grasping channel.

"Who do you belong to?" he ground out.

It took Corin a few breathless moments to stammer out, "Y-you, M-Master."

Pushing his thumb in farther, he asked again, "Who, Corin?"

"You, Master!"

The desperation in his slave's tone sent blazing trails of fire down his spine. He renewed his rhythm with increased vigor, plunging himself swiftly into the depths of Corin's hole while fisting his cock at a merciless pace.

"Please, please," Corin begged, the shimmer of tears cresting his lashes.

"Come," Markus ordered, and almost before the words were out, his boy erupted in a strangled cry, spurting ribbons of ejaculation in thick plumes. The constriction of hot muscles surrounding Markus' cock pushed him over the edge and he shouted out as his orgasm bowled through him with brute fury. Ecstasy lived in every fiber of his being as he rode the wave of his pleasure, holding tightly to his boy as Corin collapsed onto his chest. There was a brief flare of pain from the wound on his shoulder, but it quickly dissipated under Corin's damp warmth.

Fuck, he needed this. He craved everything Corin offered and all that he had to give more than his lungs needed air to breathe. When he heard his boy whisper softly against his neck, "I need you, too," he felt the shattered pieces of his heart come together in a slow mend.

"Always," he whispered back, and it was the truth.

About the Author

I have always been a lover of books, particularly those with the dichotomy of the strong alpha male and the weaker love of their life which they must rescue. After reading all I could find in M/F books, I decided to give M/M fiction a try and my addiction skyrocketed.

Hot, sexy men times two? No contest. Unfortunately, I was reading faster than the authors could produce. Eventually, I resorted to imagining my own stories and my mind took off from there.

I have to admit, though, I am a bit of a recluse. If not for the joy and humour my husband and four boys bring to me, I would never have ventured this far.

Nikki McCoy loves to hear from readers. You can find her contact information, website details and author profile page at http://www.totallybound.com.

Totally Bound Publishing